Metamorphosis

Florida Writers Association Collection,
Volume 16

Metamorphosis

Florida Writers Association Collection, Volume 16

Edited by the Florida Writers Association

Winter Park, Florida

Collection © 2024 Florida Writers Association
Individual Stories © 2024 Authors

Florida Writers Association
Winter Park, Florida
contactus@floridawriters.org
All rights reserved. No part of this publication may be reproduced, distributed, or transmitted in any form or by any means, including photocopying, recording, or other electronic or mechanical methods, without the prior written permission of the publisher, except in the case of brief quotations embodied in critical reviews and certain other noncommercial uses permitted by copyright law.

First edition: October 2024

Print ISBN: 978-1-7375305-5-8
eBook ISBN: 978-1-7375305-6-5
Library of Congress Control Number: 2024943504

Cover Design: Carol Faber
Copy Editing: Paul Iasevoli
Interior Formatting: Autumn Skye

Printed in the United States of America

Forward

Over a year ago, when the Collection 16 committee agreed on the 2024 theme metamorphosis, we expected a deluge of submissions about caterpillars and butterflies, or tadpoles growing into frogs that later turn into handsome princes. But instead, much to our surprise, the majority of submissions we received dealt with the afterlife, or forelife, or the life that's left when a loved one has left this life.

This year's Collection is filled with works that deal with the heartfelt memories left when love, relationships, and even one's own self is lost: A young Black man loses his pigmentation and has to redefine himself in Haitian society. A woman is brushed by the wings of her friend who's passed. And there's a forest filled with flowers seemingly sent by a deceased spouse.

Then there are stories of hope: A boy with Down syndrome who finds his sense of self in a Maine nighttime sky filled with stars, filled with hope. A woman working in a food pantry who learns that her problems are but minor irritations when she puts them in perspective against those who have nothing to eat.

Stylistically the prose and poetry in this book are as diverse as our membership. There are highly structured poems such as "Transmutation," and the poignant prose poem "Mammatus Theatre" filled with rhythmic language so vivid that the reader can almost feel the author's pain.

As you read this anthology of our members' best creative nonfiction, fiction, and poetry, relish in the knowledge that you're part of an organization of *writers helping writers*. And don't forget to peruse the NextGen Writers' contributions—they represent our future.

Paul Iasevoli, Collection 16 Executive Editor.

Content Advisory

Some material in this publication deals with situations and topics which may not be considered suitable for children or sensitive individuals, discretion is advised.

Table of Contents

Creative Nonfiction. ix
   Voices Along the Way by Scott Corey 1
   The Brush of Your Wing by Cheryl M. Dougherty 5
   Bonnie, Dee-Dee, and Grace by Phyllis McKinley. 8
   Moving On by Cathy Rebhun 12
   A Picture and a Dream by Susan Rivelli. 16

Fiction. 19
   Coyote Woman by Harry T. Barnes. 21
   Bread of Poets by P.K. Brent 25
   Marguerite's Awakening by Barbara A. Busenbark. 29
   The Gaping Yaw of Spring by Adeline Carson 34
   A Fork in the Road by Bob Ellis 38
   Who I Would Become by Michael Farrell 42
   Becoming by Jim R. Garrison 46
   I'm Different by Tilly Grey 49
   Dirtball by John Hope 53
   Freaky Thursday by Kelly Karsner-Clarke 57
   A Change of Heart by Michele Verbitski Knudsen. 61
   Waterbags by Anthony Malone 66
   Ghost Pirates by Meredith Martin. 70
   From Coffee Spill to Australia by George August Meier 73
   Love is Everything by Joanna Michaels 76
   Vanishing Color by Micki Berthelot Morency 80
   Metamorphosis by Mark H. Newhouse. 83
   Rotag by David M. Pearce. 87
   Something from a Small Moon by William R. Platt 91
   Masterpiece by K. L. Small 95
   The Wave by Minda A. Stephens 99
   The Timekeeper's Garden by Mike Summers 103
   One Small Act by Lynn Taylor 107

Metamorphosis

    Be Hopeful What You Wish For by Ed N. White 111

Poetry 115
    Madeira Beach Urchin by Rose Angelina Baptista 117
    For the Better by Nancy Lee Bethea 119
    Did I Know Love? by Deb Crutcher 121
    Mammatus Theatre by Madeline Izzo 123
    Transmutation by Denis O. Keeran. 125
    Manufacturing a Persona by Linda Kraus 126
    Metamorphosis by Donna Parrey 127
    Hummingbird by David Spiegel 128
    I-4 West by K.M. Stull 130
    A Loss for Words by Sylvia Whitman 131
    Coquina Beach by Robin Zabel. 132

NextGen Writers. 133
    Childhood by Perla Anderson 135
    Saul to Paul by Jace Burke. 137
    A Frog's Journey by Grayson Carpel 138
    Through the Seasons by Ebelle-Imani Creve-coeur. 139
    Nature's Gift by Sydney Crane 140
    My Basketball Career by Reece Hemmett 142
    The Seasonal Cycle by McKayla R. Lindor. 144
    Earth's Evolution by Hudson D. Lowe 146
    An Ode to Motherhood by Madeline Pesi 147
    A Caterpillar to a Butterfly by Zayba Zafar 149

Our Contributors 151

NextGen Contributors: Ages 9–17 161

Acknowledgements 165

CREATIVE NONFICTION

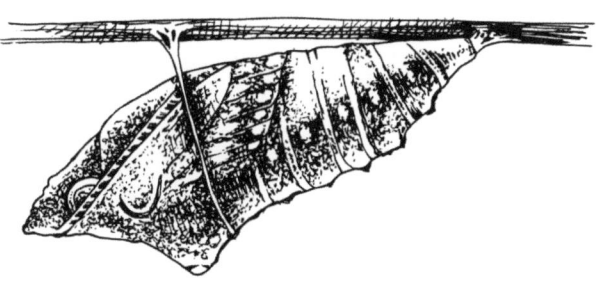

Voices Along the Way

by Scott Corey

Joël Amiot—the French author of *Le Fortin*—and I were talking about his work one afternoon when he said, "I do not speak with one voice but with many. I am every book I have ever read, every country I have visited, and every person I have known."

His comment made me think about finding my own voice as a writer: that wonderful blend of rhythm, tone, and subject which taps the deepest parts of the writer's imagination. I've always envied writers for whom voice seems to be a natural, completely effortless gift. But I say *seems*, because they no doubt put in as much patient, repetitive effort as anyone else.

When I think about how I've learned to write, I don't think about elementary school, thick pencils, or composition books. I think about a stone-white terrace in Africa, Bach's Orchestral Suite in C, a slender copy of *Go Down Moses*, and a cranky journalism professor.

In those days, I lived in West Africa and had to have an emergency appendectomy. The experience was horrifying. After surviving the operation, I convalesced at the home of an American couple.

One morning, I walked out to the terrace to enjoy the sunshine. I had rested indoors for a week and the coastal air, sunlight, and scent of mango trees in the yard lifted my spirits. I have always felt rejuvenated by being outdoors, and this time it was absolutely necessary. Clutched in one hand was a pen and a *cahier* of paper—the French kind with lines going up and down the page and across to form graph squares.

I don't remember what I was writing—perhaps a letter—when Marilyn came out to the terrace. She was carrying a cassette player and several tapes.

"I thought you might like some music," she said, smiling.

Metamorphosis

Dropping Bach's Orchestral Suite in C into the cassette player, she pressed the play button. I stopped writing and listened, captivated by the sonorous strings and flowing melody.

If only I could write like that—with that depth of intensity and rhythm and texture.

Leaning back with my eyes closed, I listened to the suite again. In fact, I played it through a dozen times during my stay. I also listened to Bach's Orchestral Suite in D, but it did not have the same effect on me as the Suite in C.

I would strive, I told myself, to capture in writing what Bach had accomplished in this musical composition.

This was step one toward finding my own voice.

The next step came a year later when my wife and I traveled upcountry on a bush truck. We had reached the railway station at Ferké when we ran into an acquaintance who was headed to the coast. As he climbed aboard the train, he tossed me a small blue book.

"What's this?" I asked.

"Faulkner," he called out. "*Go Down Moses*. I think you'll like it."

It was the Modern Library edition. I flipped randomly through the pages until I came to a story titled "The Bear." I had no idea as I skimmed the first sentence, "There was a man and a dog too this time . . ." that I was encountering a writer whose style would have a profound effect on my sense of literature and on the rhythm of my writing. Here was a style with which I could identify, a writer who had captured the essence of what I'd been trying to do with Bach. As his characters entered the wilderness of "Delta Autumn," Faulkner's writing tapped into the human spirit evident in Bach's music. I knew immediately that I had found a new friend. Slipping the narrow volume into my backpack, we continued our journey toward the savannah.

Later, when we arrived in Pindjali and washed away the perspiration and finely caked orange dust of the road, I opened the book to page one and began a serious study of Faulkner's writing style.

A few years later, we moved to Paris and spent the summer teaching at a school in Switzerland. The school was located in Montagnola, in the scenic foothills of the Swiss-Italian Alps, just down the hill from the village where Herman Hesse had lived.

I was browsing through the school library when I picked up a novel by the British writer Graham Greene. It was *The Quiet American*. The opening scene describes a beautiful Vietnamese girl, the scent of opium smoking, and yellow blossoms falling among the keys of the journalist's typewriter. And I thought, Wow!

I read the novel that summer and purchased a copy for myself as soon as we returned to Paris. I can still remember walking out of the Galignani bookstore to the covered walkway along the Rue de Rivoli with the book in my hand. If Bach's music had given me a sense of texture and intensity, and Faulkner had introduced me to a flowing, deep, Southern rhythm, then the prose of Greene gave me a tone, a world-experienced, and a cynical way of viewing life which suited my temperament.

The next stage came when we left Europe and returned to Kansas City. Up to that point, I had lived the life of an expatriate writer in France. I lingered in the cafés, with my notebook and pen, steeped in the romance of the lost generation. Writing had become like a religious experience with a capital *W*. I had to have just the right kind of paper, a pen with a thin black point, and the Parisian light filtering through the chestnut trees. Everything had to be just right.

Then I enrolled in journalism school in Kansas. Immediately, the sense of romanticism and sentimentality was knocked out of my work and head. I learned that, after all, writing was a craft like any other—not so different from carpentry or bricklaying. You learned how to do it through practice and by putting your butt onto a chair and getting the job done. All of my ridiculous notions of writing as "art" were quickly trampled in the rush to get a newspaper out on time.

One professor, a cranky, rumpled old journalist who had seemingly been around since the days of William Allen White, crunched up a reporter's assignment, tossed it angrily into a waste paper basket, and growled, "This is crap! Do it again!"

I was on the receiving end of this humiliation once and vowed it would never happen to me again. Professional writing was a craft; a job that took hard work and persistence, and I would do my best to learn it. As a result, my writing improved dramatically—or, as I liked to say, "a thousand percent."

Joël Amiot did not speak with one voice, but with many. I remembered his comment when I sat down to write my first novel. On my palette I had the texture of Bach, the rhythm of Faulkner, the tone of Greene, and the craft of journalism. All that was required for me to find my own voice now was to set these influences aside and to listen to the small inner voice, as Doris Lessing described it, which came from within.

For good or bad, this was the voice that was me.

The Brush of Your Wing

by Cheryl M. Dougherty

What is it like, my friend? To draw in that final worldly breath. To enjoy the last loving touch of your spouse and your sibling before your spirit is slowly drawn up and away from your body. Do you feel sadness or loss when you realize you will never again experience the warmth of those earthly touches? Do you sense the pain in their hearts? Does it echo in yours? Or is the joy, the anticipation of what lies ahead, so strong that it buffers any sadness?

What is it like as that instant approaches? Do you feel it coming? Is it the white-light event we have heard so much about? What happens after that drifting-away moment of your transformation?

I believe that as your soul left its earthly host, you were allowed a brief farewell tour. Our Father in Heaven let your spirit sweep the earth, catching glimpses of all the people and places you hold dear in your heart. My mind's eye can clearly see your soul soaring across the skies, swooping here and there for a closer look or a light touch. Your beautiful smile beams and your eyes sparkle with joy, lighting the way as you revisit these familiar pieces of your past. There is the spot where you met your true love, the seaside house filled with years of happy memories, the wharf where younger versions of you and I dodged seagulls who were trying to steal our clam cakes. Then you see the parent, sibling, child, or pet whose very existence filled your heart with joy, passion, laughter, tears . . . all of the deep emotions that made your life so rich. You might return to the random person whose encounter with you left an indelible mark for no particular—or a very particular—reason. You gratefully take the opportunity to remember people and places that helped mold your life. The teachers, bosses, mentors who offered constructive criticism and guidance, pointing out opportunities and opening doors to help you fulfill your dreams. You also return to the childhood friends with whom you share memories; whose visits, no matter how far in between, always felt as if you had never been apart. The visits which stirred deep affection, nonstop conversation, wonderful laughter like no other. I want to believe that this is how it is for all people of faith, but I especially believe it for a soul as beautiful as yours.

I felt your visit last night, although I did not realize it at the time. I went to bed early but tossed restlessly, my mind tangled in several threads of thought that filled me with anxiety. I tried to relax but could not. Eventually, I dozed off. Between 10:30 and 11:30, something woke me from a vivid dream, a breeze, or the brush of a feather against my shoulder. In the dream, I was writing both my obituary and my husband's. It was not frightening or even sad, yet when the brush woke me, my heart was fluttering wildly in my chest. There was no pain, just palpitations so strong that I think, even in the darkness, they would have been visible if someone had been watching. For a moment I thought I might be dying, but I was not scared. I did not understand it, but there was something familiar and safe about what was happening. Slipping from my bed so as not to wake my husband, I went to the living room and stood staring out the sliding glass doors, letting the quiet darkness of my home calm me. Not really thinking about anything, I simply absorbed what I had experienced. Later, I returned to bed and slept peacefully.

When I woke up this morning, I shared what had happened with my husband. He was fascinated by the clearness of the details but bothered by the death references. We both wondered about the reason for this unsettling experience. The responsibilities of the day eventually moved in and directed our attention to other things. This all happened hours before I found out that you had been ill, and long before I got the shocking phone call from my aunt telling me that my oldest, dearest friend had left this world during the night.

What is it like? To be free of earthly shackles? To be on the other side, in another form, gazing down at those who love you? Your joints no longer ache. Your vision and hearing are once again perfect, and your hair is not graying and coarsening. Its texture is lush and thick as it was when we were teenagers. I was always jealous of your hair. Remember how hard we laughed about these things at our last dinner together? Although our bodies told us differently, we did not want to believe that we were old enough to be experiencing the ravages of aging. The face each of us saw as we glanced across the table that night was still eight, or twelve, or at most, eighteen years old. We were not seeing the sixty-something-year-old bodies but rather the souls that bonded us as children. I imagine that your new form reflects that soul. It must be magnificent—free from illness, pain, exhaustion, grief, fear, and highlighting the absolute best of you. I envy you.

Now that I am aware of your passing, I realize it was you who woke me. You flew past, testing your new wings, and brushed me lovingly with one as you embarked on your incredible journey. You included me in the exclusive group of people, places, and experiences that you wanted to touch one last time. You took a moment to remember me and to say goodbye for now.

What is it like?

To see God? Everything He does is for a reason. He called you for something incredibly special. What is it like to know what that reason is?

Thank you, my friend, for remembering me and letting me know it. Your gesture touched me profoundly. It was a gift of love, a gift from God.

Bonnie, Dee-Dee, and Grace

by Phyllis McKinley

Highland's County sheriffs, with lights flashing and sirens blaring, stopped six lanes of traffic on Highway 27 to allow the procession to pass. We followed the silver Lincoln hearse as it led from the church to the cemetery for my husband's burial service. Traffic resumed, full speed, in all directions as soon as we were past. But I felt as if everything in my life stopped that day.

Today I noticed the grass had grown, the days were longer. Eight weeks now, and the jasmine has bloomed again; its aroma sweet on the evening air.

People talk to me about the stages of grief. I can't agree with Dr. Kubler-Ross. Denial went in the ground with the casket. It's too late to bargain. I dare not be angry with the God who carried me through many devastations. Yet to know even sadness, one has to be able to feel. Is there a word to describe when the mirror reflects only a wax replica of who you once were?

As I go through the deluge of papers required to fulfill the business of dying, I see my signature but do not remember signing. I gave the funeral director the "permission for burial." Did I really? Did I know, that in addition to my husband's body, I was burying forever life as I knew it? Was I aware of all the dreams now turned to dust? Did I consent, with one stroke of my pen, to a committal service for my identity as "wife/partner/loved one?" As the weeks pass and the numbness thaws, these paper reminders of my husband's death bring intangible pain for what is gone like the phantom pain an amputee feels for the limb no longer there.

I look for examples of beauty restored or created anew from brokenness. The blue pottery bowl, with its scars mended in gold by the art of kintsugi, invites the fingers to explore it. The delicately stitched quilt, patterned from remnants, promises warmth and comfort. The stained glass windowpane, with its perfectly cut shards, perpetually disperses light. Yes, in art and possibly in life, brokenness can be transformed into beauty. It takes vision, patience, and energy, but all I can imagine at the moment is a hollow cavern.

Meanwhile in real life, what do I do with this messy grief? I am not a pretty crier. My heart doesn't bleed in delicate rivulets. Some days it spatters; some days it spurts. Some days it sheds only a drop or two: just enough to ruin a white linen shirt. This new grief has opened up all the old griefs, all the other times when I stood by graves and watched my loved ones leave me broken, empty, lost. What will put me back together? Who will teach me to be receptive to touch again? How long before I can offer comfort and warmth to others? When will I raise the blinds that darken my soul and be able to reflect sunlight?

Each encounter with the death of one close to my heart has been an unplanned surgery that excised part of me. The more repeats, the deeper and sharper the scalpel cut. The loss of parents, brothers, sister, dearest friends, and the many aunts, uncles, and cousins of my big extended family chiseled away at my heart. With each death, another tendril of my life that had attached me to someone special was snipped off. I felt my world constrict as so many who knew me best, so many whose influence and involvement shaped my life and helped define it, were now no longer here to affirm and sustain me.

I don't think I will ever get used to death or achieve any kind of total healing from it. The emptiness it creates at its center becomes a kind of living entity that attaches itself to the soul like lichen to a tree trunk. Not only death, but the deep aches of experiences that separate, betray, or isolate us add to this painful growth. I have no hope that I can truly shed the impact of all my losses. But, through them, I have grown enough to understand that I am not defined solely by those losses.

Years ago, in less time than it took for the ambulance to arrive, a heart attack took my dad's life in the church parking lot on a frigid Christmas Eve. Four years ago, in fewer minutes than it took to book my flight home, my younger sister squeezed my hand for the last time and went to her final sleep. One year later, my brother followed her. And just eight weeks ago, in less time than the traffic stopped for the funeral procession to pass, half of my life was severed from me. The shedding part of metamorphosis can be abrupt, brutal, and shockingly permanent. We know we will never be the same again. We are right.

The grief experts advise us to get outdoors, to maintain connection with others. I have to force myself to leave the work. Do they realize how much "stuff" one person can accumulate? Do they understand how the necessary suddenly becomes the useless, the unneeded? I mull on this as I walk, mostly the same route each day, inwardly hoping I will not meet anyone. I don't want to answer that question "How are you doing?" I don't know the right answer or even the truthful one yet.

I see new neighbors have moved into Gus's place. A teenage girl sits on the step with her Labrador Retriever. I ask the dog's name. "Bonnie," she shyly replies. The girl and Bonnie do not ask me how I am doing. I like them already. I had a black Lab once, but today I'm trying to stay in the moment. I find myself surprised by colors and sounds and motions as if I've been living in a black-and-white still film for a long time. Crimson bougainvillea are in bloom; a small tree is heavy with yellowing papayas. Mourning doves call from palm to palm. An energetic white terrier races back and forth along the fence by the house on the corner. Dee-Dee no longer barks at me, just wags her tail exuberantly. I learned her name last week after she escaped her collar and ran into the street. She let me scoop her up and take her back to her owner who now secures her more carefully.

After my walk, it's a return to an empty house and sorting of thoughts along with heaping bags of stuff for Goodwill. I think of Bonnie's gentleness and Dee-Dee's delight in seeing me. And I know there's something more I need to share. I sense my heart is flooded with the love I still have for those closest to me who are now gone.

Weekends are the loneliest. I force myself out for a longer walk. My next-door neighbor drives in as I approach. His wife is expecting their second baby soon, so I inquire.

"She's in the car." He beams and invites me to meet sweet Baby Grace.

As I see the radiant mother, proud father, and a pink-and-white living doll, I glimpse life in its most exquisite tenderness. I hasten away so they can get settled. Will I ever find the words to let them know what an honor I have been granted?

Collection 16

The cracks in my heart may never heal, but I'm hoping they can allow the love in my reservoir to leak out to my neighbors and others. Seeing adorable Baby Grace, in her freshly born perfection, was a gift of spiritual grace. Through her my hope was revived, and I saw that new life will continue to sprout in me when I am willing to release the shadows of the past and welcome the colorful present, moment by vibrant moment. For me, this marks the infancy of my metamorphosis from grief to joy.

Moving On
by Cathy Rebhun

Cheerleader Christine sashayed by, short skirt swinging. Around me, shouts of kids rose and fell, locker doors clanged, and a few girls with their books held close to their chests scurried past. A paper banner strung across the ceiling announced the Spring Fling dance on Saturday, April 12, 1975, but someone had messed up, and the seven looked more like a nine. The cheerleader brushed against me before turning back with a look of disdain. "Watch where you're going, Zitface." Her haughty tone made me shrink even further into myself.

Lori came up on my other side and sighed. "Look at them."

I followed my friend's gaze to where Christine now leaned into Brad, the one everyone knew would be voted King of the Spring Fling. The cheerleader gave a loud laugh that sounded completely fake to me. When the couple kissed, I looked away.

Lori nudged me, and we headed to class.

Back in January, my first day at Conestoga High School, I'd met Lori. Every first day of school was filled with a combination of anticipation and worry: Was I wearing the right thing? Would I be able to find my classes? Would I fit in? But starting in the middle of tenth grade added an extra layer of worries. Even though I was usually friendly and outgoing, my stomach was flip-flopping with first-day nerves.

Everything in this school felt foreign—from the other kids' Philadelphia-tinged speech patterns to the clothes they wore. Even the hallways smelled different from my old high school hundreds of miles away. A hint of onions overlaid with un-mopped floors and a sprinkling of something I didn't even want to identify pervaded everything. The crowd in the hallway swept me along, and no one even looked at me.

My other high school had been equally large, but at least I knew people. Here, I was a stranger.

Late that first day, in Mr. Ramsey's Public Speaking class, a girl—her thick brown ponytail bouncing—said, "Hi, I'm Lori. You're new. Where are you from?"

"Outside Chicago," I said.

"Ohhh, me too." Lori's eyes sparkled and, now that she mentioned it, I caught the Midwestern twang. "We have to talk."

The start of class cut our conversation short, but from that moment on Lori took me under her wing. Through her, I met a small group of other girls who, like us, were studious, awkward, and not quite hip. We were definitely un-cool—one of the lowest tiers in a lengthy pecking order I didn't really understand except to know I was near the bottom. But at least there were others, including my few acquaintances and my new best friend, Lori, in the same boat. We floated along together, wolfing our lunches down in an out-of-the-way table in the far corner of the packed cafeteria, or rushing to our lockers between classes.

Lori saw a kinship in our joint Chicago background. I didn't necessarily feel the Illinois connection because I'd only lived there five years, but I believed wholeheartedly in whatever force brought us together. Our friendship felt meant-to-be. We developed a shorthand way of talking and embraced the term "dud" to describe almost everything.

"Last night's *M*A*S*H* episode was a dud," I said.

Lori pushed her glasses up her nose. "I know. It felt like watching an old-fashioned news show."

"I can't believe we have to wait till fall for the next season."

She took another bite of sandwich, her braces glinting. "Repeats are duds."

People at school were duds, too. Mr. Ramsey was a super dud. Like many classmates, I couldn't speak in front of the class without saying um a lot. To break my bad habit, Mr. Ramsey repeated every um I uttered. His distracting echo made me tongue-tied. Everyone watched my failure, and I squirmed, searching in silence for the next word. My five-minute speech, practiced at home to perfection, took fifteen in class.

Ramsey equaled super dud. Lori agreed.

Over time, Lori and I grew closer. We teamed up on a speech about Shakespeare, and in gym class we sat cross-legged in matching uniforms, trying equally hard to remain unnoticed by the girls playing a hard-core game of volleyball.

When the school year ended, Lori and I parted. She was busy with family trips. I stayed occupied with a summer reading program. We didn't see each other at all, and the summer passed in a blur.

In September, I eagerly scanned the hallways looking for Lori. A tall boy rushed by and jumped to touch a welcome-back banner stretching above our heads. The warning bell rang. I swerved around a teacher pushing a cart.

A loud giggle, instantly recognizable, came from a cluster of kids huddled in front of a locker. They shifted, revealing Christine, who wore bell-bottoms that hugged her in all the right places. She threw back her head and laughed again.

When she moved out of the way, I stopped.

Behind Christine, Lori tipped her head in a motion identical to Christine's. It took me a moment to even recognize my friend. She must have gotten contacts because her glasses were gone. Ditto her braces. Instead of the ponytail she'd previously sported, her hair shimmered past her shoulders. And she'd lost at least twenty pounds so that she probably weighed only a little more than I did, with alluring curves where I had none. Her bell-bottoms and top looked similar to Christine's but in a different color.

I approached. "Hi, Lori," I said, "you look great."

She turned my way, tossing her head. "Oh, hi." She smoothed her green polyester top. "Thanks," she said, before moving closer to a boy I didn't recognize. She gave a trilling laugh.

I cringed.

I felt my face flush and hurried to class.

For days afterward, high school—where I'd never fit in—felt stifling. Stuck in the past, I held out hope that my friend was still there, hiding under her new, glossier camouflage. Eventually, though, I had to face facts. There was no sign. Lori was gone.

When we met in the hallways, Lori managed to look past me as if I didn't exist, and I'd feel a twinge of sadness and anxiety churn deep in my gut. Our connection had snapped in two, irretrievably broken, and I had no idea what I'd done. Maybe I'd misjudged our friendship. Did we even have a real bond to begin with?

I felt alone and lost. While I sat by myself on the gym floor sidelines, I debated whether I could change too. Getting rid of my acne would make me more popular, I supposed, but even strong prescription meds had failed. Maybe I could fake some surface stuff or dress differently, although I doubted that I was a good enough actor to pull off such a switch.

I wasn't sure I'd even know how to pretend. Deep down, no matter what my appearance, I knew I'd still be me.

After much obsessing, I realized the geeky kids on the sidelines—the ones just like me—felt genuine and real in a way that cheerleader Christine never could. If Lori wanted to hang out with a dud like Christine, my old friend Lori was definitely gone. She never spoke to me again, beyond the bare minimum required by civility.

In the end, there was only one path to follow. I shook off the self-pity and chose to move on. I ended up taking an additional class in order to graduate a year ahead of schedule.

My college was smaller than my high school which made it easier to feel included. Surrounded by young people similar to me, I made new friends. Lori and the duds in high school faded into my past.

At the beginning of my sophomore year, in a so-crazy-it-can't-be-true twist, a brunette on the other side of the college cafeteria gave a high-pitched giggle. I recognized it at once. I searched for the source, and Lori turned my way. She looked right through me, just like in high school.

This time, I didn't even flinch. I'd moved on.

A Picture and a Dream

by Susan Rivelli

In my dream family and many friends surrounded me, some of whom I had not seen or thought of for years. The gathering was a Celebration of Life for my husband. In the dream, we shared hugs and laughs while telling stories of this man who was so very much missed. As the gathering ended, one by one my friends embraced me as they said their "goodbyes." When I was finally alone in this dream, I began to cry, sobbing really. When I woke, I found myself wiping real tears from my cheek. Turning to the picture on the bedside table, I kissed Pete's smiling face.

Pete and I always enjoyed traveling. We had been to Europe several times but had never toured France, so one year we booked a trip that would take us from Paris, through Normandy's beaches of World War II, and the Loir Valley. The plan was to go in April 2020. But then, COVID stunned the world. Our trip was canceled along with much of life as everyone knew it. But we survived COVID-19 and its unfortunate aftereffects. We rebooked the trip for April 2023. However, by the time February rolled around, it had become clear that my husband was no longer able to travel to Europe or anywhere for that matter. The cancer that had dogged him on and off for years reared its ugly head for the umpteenth time. This time, the cancer prevailed. Once again, the France tour was canceled.

Pete's health declined gradually over the next months. Our roles transitioned during that time. For our thirty-five-plus years together, it was always Pete taking charge. He always knew what needed to be done and then made sure it got done. While a new, unfamiliar role as head of household leaped into my hands, it was frightening and heartbreaking, to say the least, watching this once strong, confident, and determined man becoming weaker each day and dependent on others. For me, the role of full-time caregiver turned out to be the most difficult job of my entire seventy years.

On November 3, 2023, Pete was surrounded by his four favorite girls—our three daughters and me. Huddled together by his side, holding his hands while praying, the once vibrant, handsome man, whom I had fallen in love with some thirty-seven years before, took his final breath. I kissed his forehead one last time.

When a spouse dies, the surviving spouse finds their life changed in an instant. No matter how prepared one might be, the loss is deeply felt. That is what happened to me as I began my grieving journey of sadness, confusion, numbness, and loneliness. Even with the support of family and friends, I still felt a hole in my heart that I doubt will ever fully heal. Strangely though, while I felt my heart breaking, tears never came. Although I felt pain internally, I could not let it be revealed on the outside.

I filled the weeks following the funeral by going about the business that needs to occur when someone dies. Days were spent tending to financial, personal, and legal issues. It was exhausting, but staying busy let me forget my loss for a time. It was during this time, while going through the plethora of emails, one email popped up promoting a France tour. This was the same tour Pete and I had booked twice before, and it was again available in April! Was this divine intervention? I did not know nor care at that moment. With little hesitation, I contacted the travel agent and booked the trip.

"We're finally going to France, Pete!" I grinned at that familiar face in the small, framed photo above the mantel; that beautiful face with those twinkling eyes that always smiled back. I was thrilled at first, but then apprehension snuck in. I would be traveling solo to a different country, another continent away, for the very first time. Was I just being impulsive and extravagant in my grief? Too late now.

Five months later, I sat in my assigned seat on a Boeing jet flying from Tampa to Paris. But I was not alone. I pulled the framed photo from my carry-on. This picture was the one he had chosen months ago to include in his obituary. It was a photo he had taken some years ago, before his body had turned against him. When he was still strong. When that handsome smile and those twinkling eyes had not faded. Before the ugly ravage of cancer swallowed him up. Now, I sat the picture on the small table above my lap where it stayed throughout the overseas flight. I was determined that Pete would share every moment of this journey with me.

Upon arrival in Paris, I met up with the tour group. We spent several nights there before moving on to explore more of France. We visited the beaches of Normandy, castles and chateaus in the Loir Valley, and the homes of Monet and of DaVinci. We tasted sweet French wine and delicacies. After a week of traveling by bus, enjoying the sites, and admiring the beautiful French countryside, we returned to Paris for the final night. The group joined in a champagne toast to honor Pete at our last dinner together. I showed them the picture I had brought with me, setting it near me each night in the hotel rooms.

Upon falling asleep that final night in Paris, I dreamt of family and friends celebrating Pete's life and, after everyone left, I cried in the dream and on my pillow. After a while when I awoke, I understood that the trip had allowed me to finally release the tears I had contained for so long. The dream symbolized to me an ending to the life I had known—my crying bringing forth essential healing.

On the drive along the Seine that morning heading to Charles de Gaulle Airport, I recalled the dream. The tears had long dried, and sadness had been replaced with a sense of peace. It struck me that this trip was not simply a spur-of-the-moment indulgence. I needed to go on the trip, and I needed to have Pete with me, even if only in a picture. This trip was an opportunity for closure. I felt blessed to have had a final shared journey with my husband but had now reached a point where it was okay to move on. I tucked the picture in my carry-on. I smiled, knowing he was looking down at me and smiling back with his beautiful, broad smile.

FICTION

Coyote Woman

by Harry T. Barnes

A filigree of frost crystals on my camper window sparkled with sunlight as morning came to the spruce forest where I'd spent the night. From the warmth of my down sleeping bag, I poked out a long-underwear-clad arm and clicked on the propane Buddy heater.

I had spent the night on Rattlesnake Mountain in the Colorado Rockies where at 4,000 feet elevation, although it was mid-May, the temperature had dropped to twenty-eight degrees. Thirty miles below, in the hippy hamlet of Patchouli Gap, it would be in the fifties.

I retrieved the water bottle from my sleeping bag, where I had kept it from freezing, and boiled water for coffee on my Jetboil camp stove. Once the windshield ice melted, I cautiously maneuvered my VW camper down the steep winding mountain road to Patchouli Gap and the Ouray Café, which opened at six a.m. every day except for Bob Marley's birthday, February 6, considered locally as a national holiday.

Komeha Montoya, the dark-eyed young woman behind the counter, must have thought I looked like a frozen logger with my wool mittens, heavy wool jacket, collar up around my ears, and dusty cowboy hat pulled low. "Looks like you could use a coffee, cowboy." She smiled, then returned to making change for a customer. "There's a table up front . . . there by the window." She motioned with her chin; her high cheek bones and dark complexion catching the morning light.

I acknowledged my gratitude by touching the brim of my black cowboy hat purchased for five bucks at a thrift store in Del Rio, Texas. During my yearlong walkabout out west, I had found that pearl-button chambray shirts, faded jeans, cowboy boots and hat helped me feel like I belonged.

Metamorphosis

After eggs, hash browns, grits, toast, and a third refill of coffee, I flipped my hat on, fiddled it in place, and went to pay Komeha. As I waited in line to pay, I noticed a display case of flint-knapped projectile points and stone tools, then walked over to admire them.

Fascinated by the craftsmanship and archaic origin of the pieces, I was kneeling on the old plank floor when Komeha leaned over the counter; her raven braids flopping on the countertop. "My uncle's collection," she said. "He's been collecting since he was a boy. He owns this place."

With the velvet-skinned woman smiling down on me, her face only inches away, arrowheads forgotten, I got lost in those deep, dark eyes. When the smile on her red lips grew broader, I felt my face turn red—hopefully hidden by my full beard.

After I composed myself, I stood and handed over my Discover card. As she ran the card, I asked about the local hot spring I'd heard about. I never pass up a hot spring and looked forward to a good long soak.

"You mean Hell Hole," she said. "Yeah, it's up on Rattlesnake Mountain about five miles out of town. Hard to find though."

"Hell Hole?" I asked.

"Yeah, it is hot as hell and stinks of sulfur. Get it?"

"Got it."

Pointing to her name tag, I said, "Unusual name."

From behind me, a tall fellow also with Native American features, grinned at Komeha and said, "Means 'Coyote Woman, the trickster.' Gotta watch her every minute."

"My cousin," she explained, rolling her eyes. "Don't pay Warren no mind, he couldn't tell a coyote from a prairie dog. "Truth is, in Ute legend, Komeha, or Coyote Woman, was a medicine woman, a healer, who had a deep understanding of nature's ways and human behavior."

"So, Coyote Woman, you must know the way to Hell Hole."

"Best way is on horseback," she said. "There's a trail—head five miles west of Patchouli, but there's no place to park and no trail sign, so it's hard to find."

Not sure what gave me the gumption, it just came right out. "What time you get off?"

"Why do you ask?"

"I don't know, thought maybe I could buy you a beer, or a burger, or something." I paused, then spat out, "Maybe you'd show me Hell

Hole." I pasted a smile on my face with eyebrows raised and waited. Her unsmiling, steady stare was disconcerting. I felt my face heat up again but held her gaze.

"You don't talk like a cowboy," she said. "Where are you from?"

Realizing my costume had not fooled her, I shrugged and confessed. "Nowhere special, just ramblin'."

"Vagabond, huh. Searcher. Lonely life," she said, suddenly appearing older and wiser than her thirty-something years.

At two o'clock that afternoon, when Komeha got off work, she took me to see her uncle at his ranch a mile outside the Gap. The craggy, bright-eyed old man showed me his pre-Puebloan artifacts and regaled me with his knowledge of local nature and Western history. After mugs of strong dark coffee and homemade cinnamon buns, her uncle took us to the barn where Komeha stabled her paint quarter horse, White Cloud. He picked out a docile dun mare for me that he said was trail savvy and well behaved and that I was welcome to borrow.

The ride from the ranch to Hell Hole was six miles of steep, rock-strewn mountain trails. After an hour aboard my sure-footed mare, the jostling and jerking had my thighs and butt cheeks on fire. "How much farther?" I asked.

"Saddle sore, cowboy?" She grinned. When she had asked if I could ride, of course I said yes, thinking, *how hard can it be?* I wished now that we were walking.

At a wide sandy spot in a canyon, Komeha reined in and dismounted. "Horses need a blow," she explained. "Spring's not far now. Should smell sulfur soon."

I gingerly slid from my saddle, glad for the respite, and took a long swig from my water bottle.

After crisscrossing a small stream several times, we arrived in a meadow below a steep cliff where a waterfall dropped twenty feet into a pool of water. On the left side of the pool, a cloud of steam revealed the spring's location.

Komeha tied our horses to a makeshift hitching rail and hung her hat on the saddle horn. Unabashed, she peeled off her plaid shirt, unfastened her bra, and placed them on a log. Once we were both naked and ready for our immersion in Hell Hole, Komeha took the small silver amulet she wore on a rawhide cord around her neck and unscrewed the tiny cap. "Peyote opens the mind and heart to the spirit within," she said. After taking a sip herself, she passed it to me. I hesitated only a moment, then took a sip as she had.

    Hand in hand we walked the stone pathway to the inferno. Timidly testing with our toes, soon we were in up to our necks. Healing heat, soothing sulfur, and a potion of peyote worked their magic in the ethereal mist. Clinging to one another to keep from swooning, we glided to the stone-ringed bank and sat together waist deep, mesmerized, peaceful, happy. Drowsy and grinning, we kissed and embraced, Hell Hole—too hot for much more.

    Then out of the steam a vision appeared. At first, we thought we were dreaming—a gray-bearded man and a woman, likewise wizened, stood smiling at us from afar.

    At the old woman's throat hung a silver amulet that looked like a coyote.

Bread of Poets

by P.K. Brent

Aunt Julie stood up, smoothed her smock, and rapped her knuckles on the edge of the control panel.

"You all know the special reason why we're meeting in video today."

Stacy squirmed in her seat, wondering what was going on, trying not to glance at Aunt Julie's twin daughters—Amanda and Abigail—who were whispering together and eyeing boxes on a table behind them. Even though they were off-worlders, the twins were dressed in impeccable teen fashions, with hair in glossy curls, sporting cerulean blue fingernails. Stacy's nails were stubby due to numerous research projects. She hid her stubby nails in her lap and squirmed in her everyday slacks and baggy smock.

"The family reunion is next Terra-moon here on ColonyX2B. Many relatives will attend. I've arranged comfortable pods and have a full schedule of events planned. We will honor a particular ancestor, as we do at every reunion. It's important to keep Terran customs and family ties alive. After all, we are mammals. This type of humanoid social behavior helps regulate serotonin and dopamine." Aunt Julie worked as a neurologist and always was concerned with brain chemicals and bodily rhythms.

"This year we will honor your great-grandmother Murray, whom you've never met. Nonetheless, a special contest for you four is planned. Great-grandma Murray was an excellent cook, but she lived during the Dim-Ages and never recorded a recipe. My sister, your aunt Louisa, and I have been able to recreate all her recipes except one: her Irish soda bread. We're close, but it isn't quite right. As a special project, we hope that you four—Grandma Murray's great-grandchildren—can figure it out."

"I'm not going to bake bread," sneered Jacob, Aunt Louisa's son.

"You wouldn't win anyway," Abigail pointed out. "Amanda and I have been designing food for years in FoodX Club, so we're sure to win."

"If I were to bother, I would beat you two . . . no problem. I can make anything in the Junior Molecular Chemistry Lab," replied Jacob.

Aunt Julie ignored the interruption. "Whoever comes up with the recipe closest to Great-grandma Murray's wins a prize." Aunt Julie held up a box featuring a turquoise tablet, not just any tablet but the new Corona V Pro. Jacob's mouth dropped open. He was nearly drooling. The twins grew quiet. Stacy felt pure desire coursing through her body. The things she could do with that tablet!

"I'll be the winner," boasted Jacob. "With chemistry, I know how to analyze molecular components. That tablet is mine!"

"Amanda and I have designed dozens of food formulas in FoodX Club, and we have access to the best food simulator available. We will win for sure!"

"I don't think it's fair that the twins team up," Jacob pointed out.

"Why would you care?" asked Amanda.

"We would share the tablet," added Abigail.

Stacy remained quiet, listening to her cousins fuss over the prize. Clearly her cousins believed she was no competition at all, just because she remained on the worn home planet of Terra, but Stacy was confident in her research ability. She was already looking up recipes for Irish soda bread from the Dim-Age on her comphone.

"Do you have anything to add, Stacy?" asked Aunt Julie. Stacy looked up from her research.

"I will do my best," replied Stacy.

Jacob sneered, and the twins rolled their eyes.

Aunt Julie continued, "Years ago, Aunt Louisa searched Great-grandma Murray's pod on the primitive outpost of Asteroid5UY, looking for valuables and antiques. Some of these items were kept in storage until recently. There are few modern conveniences on Asteroid5UY. Most work was done manually, the way humanoids worked two hundred years ago. Three boxes of antique equipment were saved—one box for each team. The boxes contain baking pans, bowls, spoons, sifters, old-fashioned measuring cups, and items called teaspoons, among other things. I suggest you research this equipment on the Inter-Galactal Web and learn how to use it. You can manufacture ingredients with the FoodX Simulator or in a Molecular Chemistry lab, but you must mix and bake the primitive way. Primitive ovens are available here on ColonyX2B in the Recreation Center. Stacy, your father will find you a primitive oven to use, which should not be a problem on Terra."

Groans from Jacob and the twins were audible. Aunt Julie ignored the sounds of discontent.

"One box for each team is on the table behind me. Choose one, lock on, and transport it to your DeliverX Chamber." Jacob and the twins remotely viewed the contents of the boxes, quickly chose, and transported their chosen box. Stacy looked up from searching Irish soda bread recipes to see that only one box remained. She fumbled with the DeliverX controls and, a few seconds later, a box of antique baking supplies appeared in front of her.

Stacy poked through the box of baking tools, looked each item up on the Inter-Galactal Web, and read how to use it. She was engrossed in research when her father entered the room.

"I hear my sisters have a primitive baking contest for you kids."

"Yes. At the reunion next Terra-moon, Aunt Louisa will do a taste-test and whoever makes the Irish soda bread closest to Great-grandma Murray's will win a new Corona V Pro tablet."

"Wow! That's exciting. Nice prize."

"Yes, but I got the junkiest box of equipment. I saw that my cousins had all newer things in their boxes, even white rectangular baking pans. Look at this piece of junk!" Stacy held up a dented, round metal pan that sported a little rust.

"That's the exact pan she used! I remember it. That pan was old and dented when I was a boy."

"Did you ever eat the soda bread?"

"Yes. Unlike my sisters, who deplore primitive accommodations, I enjoyed visiting my Grandma Murray on Asteroid5UY. Her soda bread was very good."

"What else do you remember about it?"

"She baked it in that pan. Once it cooled, she wrapped it in a silvery paper called foil they had back then and put a green ribbon around it. Grandma Murray brought it to every communal supper and gave it to anyone who had a new baby or death in the family."

Stacy considered these facts, and it dawned on her—this Irish soda bread was important and used to honor important events in the community. It wasn't just something to eat.

"Anything else?"

Her father pondered. "She always sliced an *X* across the top before baking it."

"Why?"

"So the fairies could get out."

"What?" Stacy raised her voice, incredulous.

Her father shrugged. "That's what she said. It's hard to explain . . . people were more poetic in those times."

Stacy pointed to small metal containers with screw-on lids. Do you know what's in those? I see brown powders, and each one smells different."

Her father unscrewed the vials and gave the names one by one—cinnamon, allspice, and *cormoram* . . . no that's not right. She called it cardamon. These are spices . . . the real deal . . . not simulated."

"Secret ingredients!" replied Stacy. "No wonder the aunts could never recreate this recipe."

"A FoodX Simulator can make cinnamon and maybe even allspice. But I'm sure it can't make cardamon. Even though they're old, they smell strong, so I bet they still work."

"Is it cheating that my box came with spices?"

Her father considered Stacy's question. "Your cousins could have chosen this box. They left the junkiest equipment for you. I think you're even."

Next month on ColonyX2B, at the family reunion, just before the laser tag game started, Aunt Louisa announced the judging of the soda bread. All the relatives gathered around the table where three loaves of Irish soda bread sat. Two were rectangular. One was round with an *X* in the middle.

The twins pointed at Stacy's round bread and snickered. "Why the *X*?"

"To let the fairies out," replied Stacy.

In fits of giggles, the twins collapsed onto chairs.

"That's ridiculous," replied Jacob

Stacy stood strong. "It's poetry from a different age, about a different type of bread that's more than food. Irish soda bread nourishes bodies and souls and strengthens community ties."

Aunt Louisa brushed a crumb from her lips. "Stacy's bread is authentic in taste, appearance, and—dare I say—spirit. Great-grandma Murray would be pleased. Stacy is the winner!"

Marguerite's Awakening

by **Barbara A. Busenbark**

The rhythm of the days drummed on. Sister Catherine stood in the doorway of the girls' dormitory, wielding a tarnished brass bell. It clanged mercilessly as she raised and lowered it every day at six a.m. The forty orphans responded with moans and yawns. The smell of simmering oatmeal greeted the girls in the dining hall. Single file, they lined up, bowls in hand. She served the tasteless gelatinous goo from a large black cauldron parked on a table.

Before Marguerite turned three years old, her mother died. Mrs. Dugan lived next door and took her in along with her older sister Mary. Six months later, Mrs. Dugan could no longer care for the girls and brought them to St. Vincent's Orphanage Asylum. The year was 1903.

"Be good girls," Mrs. Dugan said as though she'd return for them. She never did.

Marguerite often asked Mary to share her memories at bedtime.

"Mother had long and dark hair, like yours. During the day, she tied it up. I loved to brush her hair at night when she let it down. Mother came from France. Father helped her learn to speak English. Sometimes she would say things in French first and then in English."

"What about Father?"

"He came from Ireland. When Mother died, he was very sad. He used to say, 'Someday I'll take you girls to Ireland, and you can see how beautiful it is there. Green hills as far as the eye can see.' He looked so happy when he talked about Ireland."

One morning, Sister Elizabeth told Mary, "Mr. Darrach and his sisters need household help. You need to be ready to leave tomorrow morning."

Metamorphosis

The thought of leaving Marguerite broke Mary's heart. Mary bolstered herself and told Marguerite the news.

"Sister Elizabeth is taking me to my new job. I won't be living here with you anymore."

"Will I ever see you again?"

"Yes, yes, don't even think that."

With one last hug, Mary walked out the door. Marguerite ran to the window to see Mary turn, wave goodbye, then disappear around the corner. Marguerite waved back and frantically wiped the condensation off the glass, trying to get another glimpse of her sister, but to no avail.

The pain of living without Mary cut into the fabric of Marguerite's being. Without her sister, Marguerite struggled to find her place in the world. The last thread that connected her to family had stretched beyond her reach.

Before Marguerite surrendered to despair, Sister Catherine rang the bell, signaling the start of sewing class. Marguerite dried her eyes, threw her shoulders back, took a deep breath, and marched down the hall determined to endure. She loved sewing—it allowed her to create something new, and this day she needed it more than ever.

The next morning, Sister Elizabeth ushered in a new girl who stared blankly at the floor. Marguerite wanted to protest the rush to give away Mary's bed—until she recognized the despondent look on her young roommate's face. The steady flow of orphans couldn't be curtailed.

"Marguerite, this is Bridgette," announced Sister Catherine.

Bridgette looked up without smiling or speaking. Everyone arrived at St. Vincent's with the same vacant expression.

"Marguerite, will you show Bridgette around?"

"Yes, Sister."

Once alone, Marguerite tried her best to comfort Bridgette.

"How old are you, Bridgette?"

"Seven."

"It's not so bad here, except for the oatmeal, oh, and the chicken pudding . . . yuck. The macaroni and cheese is okay. It's about the only thing that's okay. Just don't drop your pencil on the floor in Sister Elizabeth's class. It drives her nuts."

Bridgette's eyes widened. Marguerite had said too much and softened her tone.

"Just stick with me. You'll be fine."

"How long have you been here?"

"Ten years. My sister and I came here when our mother died."

"Where's your sister?"

"She went to work for a family."

Bridgette looked at her bed with raised eyebrows.

"Yeah, that was her bed." Marguerite's cheerfulness started slipping away.

"I'm sorry."

"Oh, that's okay. Maybe the food's better where she is." Marguerite smiled more easily. Comforting Bridgette bolstered Marguerite's confidence. "Come on, I'll show you where things are. At least we get to be late for school."

"I've never been to school."

"Before you know it, you'll be reading and writing like crazy."

A month later, Sister Elizabeth came for Marguerite. She had learned how to cook and sew and how to read and write. At thirteen, work as a servant girl loomed ahead of her. She knew nothing of the world outside or what to expect. The walls of the orphanage had surrounded and protected Marguerite like a cocoon.

"The Bermans are looking for housekeeping help. Are you ready for the job?" Sister Elizabeth asked.

"Yes, Sister."

"I'll come for you tomorrow after breakfast. Have your things together."

As Marguerite started packing, she looked up at Bridgette. "Bridgette, don't look so sad. You'll be fine." But Marguerite remembered when Mary left and understood the feeling of being abandoned.

"I don't want you to leave," Bridgette pleaded.

"You'll make friends, and somebody will take my place before you know it."

Bridgette forced a smile. Marguerite smiled back. Like the day Bridgette arrived, Marguerite felt better about herself when she cheered her young friend.

"Give me a hug, and wish me luck."

Bridgette got up and threw her arms around Marguerite's waist. The fierce grip told Marguerite more than words ever could. Tears welled up in her eyes, but she refused to give in to the sadness. The little girl who clung so tightly treated Marguerite like a big sister. That shift from being the needy one to the protector gave Marguerite strength. She loosened Bridgette's arms and kissed her on the forehead.

"You're stronger than you know. You'll find that out someday, like I did." Then Marguerite picked up her bag and joined Sister Elizabeth standing at the door.

The streets of Philadelphia surged with activity. The rumble of trolly wheels, whirs of automobile engines, and the clip-clopping of horses's hooves grew louder as they walked to the trolley stop.

"Mrs. Berman will tell you your duties. Remember your manners, and I'll tell her how good your sewing skills are."

The trolley came to a stop. Sister Elizabeth reached into the pocket of her habit and pulled out an envelope and two nickels. She handed one to Marguerite.

"Give the gentleman your fare," Sister Elizabeth said, nodding at the conductor standing by the door. Once aboard, she gestured at the first two empty seats.

"We're going to West Philadelphia. We should be there soon," said Sister Elizabeth. "And I have this for you." She handed a letter to Marguerite. "It's from Mary."

Marguerite's face lit up as she ripped open the envelope. While she read, Sister Elizabeth continued, "Mary is three blocks away from the Bermans."

"Can I see her?" Marguerite asked.

"Of course, you could go to Sunday Mass together."

Pure joy took flight. Marguerite's smile covered her face. As she stared out the window, her lingering fear of losing Mary dissipated, and a new world unfolded. Row houses lined the streets along with shops, taverns, and apartment buildings.

Sister Elizabeth stood and announced, "This is our stop."

Collection 16

Marguerite emerged from the trolley. Market Street buzzed with energy. Store clerks swept the sidewalks in front of their shops. Trolleys, horses, and cars seemed to maneuver for position on the crowded road. The elevated train startled Marguerite as it screeched around the bend above their heads.

At first it appeared chaos ruled the street, but Marguerite realized everything had its place. The choreography of people, horses, and machinery stepped in time to a well-rehearsed rhythm. Marguerite watched in awe as well-dressed pedestrians passed barking street vendors and chanting newspaper boys. A unique harmony caressed the air as the sounds melded together.

Sister Elizabeth turned onto Chestnut Street. "Here we are."

Front porches guarded by white spindled railings and peaked roofs that pointed to bow windows looked cozy and welcoming. Marguerite's world changed when she looked at the house where she'd be living. Everything would be different now.

The once-scared little girl became an independent young lady when freed from the orphanage. Life began anew for Marguerite.

The Gaping Yaw of Spring

by Adeline Carson

They would tell each other he'd touched her wrong. That was what they'd tell each other once the sticky July rains washed away the dirt she was so tediously repairing, trying not to let the bulge of his bloated remains show through.

She wondered if it was even worth the effort. And it was effort. Ever since she was a little girl, they'd called her skin and bones. She didn't think she'd ever done so much labor in all her life till this night right here, this gaping yaw of a spring night with no moon, only the resilient stars to light her way.

She wondered if she oughtn't have brought the shovel, if they might bring him up sooner than she hoped because of the way it had cut unnaturally into the dirt.

She wondered how she would look in the papers when they caught her, if the people of Oak Notch would find her a pretty murderess.

She didn't think of the chance, as slim as herself, that they wouldn't ever trace her. There were a hundred thousand small towns just like Notch in the American Midwest, and none of them was easy to get lost in. People like her had no interest in protecting the interests of those who were not their own, and too little happened in these places not to bank on every little chance you got to be a part of something bigger than yourself.

The hardest part would be convincing anyone around her that Abraham had gone missing of his own accord. Her husband was a lively and respected man; one of Notch's brightest, even though he was poor and more often unwashed than not. He had friends in church and friends at the bar, and this was unfortunate because Abraham was the kind of man who could bridge the differences between the two. His disappearance could, at least.

She would say that he had been drinking at home these past few weeks. As she hiked her muddy cream skirt above her knee and kicked the shovel deep into the dirt, she thought she would say that he'd been "wistful" and "unfocused." The girls in town at least would know what that meant.

Perhaps she did have that going for her: Abraham's incessant, irrepressible desire to charm the pants off everyone he ever met. It could be possible he charmed someone a little bit too much and fell into some trouble with some girl not from around here. He was a traveling salesman during the summer—he'd met all sorts of the kind no one in Oak Notch could claim to understand. That alone made her vague excuse almost too easy.

The only problem that had no answer she could easily divine was, of course, that Abraham had truly loved her.

It made all her joints ache and her belly reel with nausea to think of it. All truths would do this to her now. It seemed now that she was a full-blown liar for a living, a bona fide sinner right down to the bone.

It was why she couldn't trust that her tears and sham worry would hold off Abraham's buddies for long. The most doggish of his kennel probably wouldn't be put off the scent from the start. She knew what went on in those places he frequented whenever he was home and couldn't stand to look at her any longer. She'd always known, but she even had gone so far as to confirm it one night when she sneaked out after him and lounged around outside the barroom window, listening to him ache and moan over how his lovely wife had never even tried to love him back.

The specifics were not important. The core of the truth remained.

Hurling dirt over Abraham's wide green eyes, she fancied that somewhere along the line the piece of her that could have loved a man like him had just broken off.

She'd broken a plate once, one of the good set her mother had given her as a wedding present, just to see how the porcelain would come undone, if it would split into large chunks all at once or explode into slivers as small as the crescents of white on her little fingers. Turns out, it had done a little bit of both.

That was how she thought of the story of her marriage now in the belly of the darkness all around her. The winding disrepair had been slivers for awhile: little pieces chipped away from her sanity and her patience and her respect for the past three years. A soft salesman's hand at her shoulder, coaxing her to turn and face the panting mouth that awaited her own, or the smell of coffee in the morning that she couldn't help but despise because he never got hers with milk just the way she liked. She couldn't have pinpointed the first tiny fragments if she tried. All she knew was that they had always been there, no matter how small.

Then came the big shattering—his unexpected surprise. Actually, it was two big ones, come to think of it. First, he arrived home two days before she'd expected him; two precious days and nights when she would have been alone to do her weaving and her sweeping and her laughing in the spring winds all on her blessed lonesome. All right, fine. She could put up with the dashing of her expectations this once. Lord knew he'd be gone again before the week was out, this weather being so fine for traveling and all.

But then he had the gall to ask about the baby.

There was no baby in the first place, get that straight. She'd only told him so before he left this time to get his canoodling off her back. "I couldn't possibly," she'd explained lightly while his hands had fondled with her underskirt, "because then we might get hurt."

His eyes had flickered and shone when he realized the "we" she meant. It had kept him away from her for over two weeks, all his trips home combined. But that had been almost three months ago, and the evidence of her lie—or perhaps more so the lack of its truth—had started to show.

The thought of him begging her for updates made her toes curl now. If only that had been all it caused her in the moment.

At the time, she'd whirled on him with her second favorite kitchen knife still in hand. And with a sneer as cold and as cruel as the one on her father's face the day they'd come to take him away, she told him to forget it, that she'd lost the "poor dear" in the night while he'd been working. That she didn't even think of it now and neither should he, because she was never going to let it happen again.

It had felt wonderful to say all of that to his poor, handsome, pallid face. She'd returned to chopping his steak with a glow on her face, a breathless rush coming all over her in the face of her own courage.

But then she'd heard him crying.

And she knew she just couldn't take it a second more.

In the hulking shadows underneath no moon, she wondered how smoothly her first favorite kitchen knife would've slipped through his throat. Her second favorite already did so well.

She would tell them he'd up and left her for another woman, and she would pine and simper after him till the summer when she'd pack her bags and announce her intention to go on after him and bring him back. It was a boring story, really. Happened every day in the American Middle. And none of those wives ever came back either, running out of money, or time, or luck somewhere along the way.

By July she'd be well on her way to somewhere else—one of the big proper states, the ones that ate up women like her alive. She rather fancied the idea. She thought she'd like to try being eaten.

Yes, they'd tell themselves he'd touched her wrong and earned what come his way in return. Even some of his most devout friends might learn to believe it, with time.

She wondered what her mother would think and whether she would let herself believe it too.

A Fork in the Road
by Bob Ellis

Seventy miles east-northeast of Dallas stands the sleepy little city of Marshall, Texas. The downtown, populated with squat three- and four-story office buildings, broils daily under late summer's fiery East Texas sun.

Marshall's commerce primarily consists of lumber harvested from the surrounding piney woods and gushing oil wells that stab the land like porcupine quills. And every Friday, the First National Bank of Marshall, the biggest bank in town, receives a truckload of cash from the Federal Reserve in Dallas to fund the local companies' payrolls for their hard-working roustabouts and loggers.

"Wild Bill" Estes had been studying the First National's routine, inside and out, for three weeks. Fifteen minutes after the Brink's armored car from Dallas departed, seven tellers and five officers began parceling out the cash on the counting table behind the teller line.

On this last Friday in September, three raw-boned, lanky fellas strolled into the bank like they were swaggering into a saloon. They were James Doolittle, recently released from the medium-security prison down in Lumberville, "Snake" O'Connor, a Muskogee from up in Oklahoma, and Estes.

The bankers barely looked up from their count until the three men presented their particulars, two six-shot Colts and an old army .45. The blue steel so impressed the twelve bankers they stopped counting and started reaching for the sky or, at least, the fluorescent-lit ceiling.

Estes, leader of the marauders, barked his orders at the oldest, baldest, roundest banker: branch manager Fortnum Beaufort, who instructed the other bankers to immediately re-bag the freshly delivered bills. Scorning

Collection 16

the remaining cash on hand in favor of the quick getaway, the robbers grabbed the re-stuffed canvas bags and headed for the door.

"Everybody down," yelled Doolittle, firing a shot into the coffered tin ceiling. Holding their guns in one hand and the canvas bags in the other, the outlaws raced out of the bank. The trio had just pulled the biggest bank heist in East Texas history, scoring $350,000.

Stuffing the bags into a stolen gold-green '68 Impala, the robbers jumped in alongside. Wild Bill cautiously drove out of town on a route that took them back down Grand Avenue. As they passed the bank, a foolish head poked out the front entrance. Doolittle unloaded five shots from the .45, shattering the bank's smoky glass doors.

Over at the Cowtown Diner, patrons swiveled to view the man in uniform sitting at the counter. Deputy Walter Grimes, pissed that his grits and coffee were fixin' to be interrupted by the ruckus, dropped his spoon in the grits, took a swig of the lukewarm coffee, then slid off his stool.

Loping outside, Deputy Grimes squeezed off all six shots from his Colt Python at the fleeing Impala. Five missed the vehicle, but one managed to pierce the back window and make a neat hole in the back of James Doolittle's head.

Six miles farther on, in the Winn Dixie parking lot, the robbers pulled up beside a black '79 Trans Am. Snake and Wild Bill transferred the cash and guns to the Pontiac.

"We just gonna leave him like that?" asked Snake.

"He ain't going nowhere ever again," Wild Bill observed.

Following another two hours of conservative driving to attract a minimum of attention, all the while anxiously checking for pursuers, the two remaining robbers arrived at a downtown Texarkana parking garage. They proceeded up to the deserted top level.

"You crafty son of a bitch," chortled Snake. "Instead of having to split the loot three ways, now we only got to divide it in two!"

"What are we going to do for a vehicle for you? We've got to split up," said Estes. "They'll be looking for the two of us once they find Doolittle. I reckon we got about a two-hour head start on the cops."

"Guess I'll just stick with you, the Trans Am, and the money," answered the easy-going Snake. "Later, we'll relieve some citizen of their vehicle. What a haul—gotta be a hundred grand a piece!"

"That's sorta what I expected you to say," said Wild Bill, gazing through the dusty windshield at the scrubby buildings of downtown Texarkana. He looked down at the Firebird decal on the hood of the Trans Am, then back at Snake. "They're going to be watching for two guys traveling together. We have to split up."

"Can't be helped. I don't got a car yet. Don't worry, they don't know about the Trans Am. Damn it, Bill, I can't get to figuring how a smart Yankee wound up down here in East Texas giving lessons in robbing banks. Where you from again?" Snake spit out the open window for emphasis.

"Cortland, New York," said Estes, staring far across the city toward the distant prairie culminating in a Nebraska town where a girl was waiting. She would wait forever.

"Born there, went to high school and some college there, too. It was an accident . . . me winding up out here. I was driving my old Dodge Cornet, making for New York City, fixin' to go there and make a pile of money. Going south on I-81, I came to a fork, the one at Route 17. Didn't know which exit to take; one went to New York City, the other west. Having to think quick speeding at seventy, I veered left. I always wondered how things woulda turned out if I'd taken the other one."

"I reckon you'd have ended up about the same," Snake said philosophically. "It ain't the roads we take; it's our innards that makes us do what we do."

They eased out of the Trans Am for a quick stretch. Texarkana was a twin for Marshall, equally squat and dusty. "I'd be a good deal happier if we split up," said Bill softly, picking a small piece of Doolittle's remains from his vest. He flicked it over the edge into space.

Snake spat over the side of the garage and watched it drop the four stories. He was growing tired of this argument; it was time to move. When he turned and looked over the top of the car, he found himself staring into the dark, round muzzle of Bill's Colt six-shooter.

"Cut the shit, Bill. We gotta get going."

"We ain't going nowhere together," replied Estes. "I already done told you; we're splitting up."

"We's partners. Don't do nothing you'll regret," whined Snake.

"I feel pretty bad about this," replied Bill. He squeezed the trigger twice and blew O'Connor backward across two parking slots. The shots echoed around the concrete parking garage; a whiff of cordite hung in the stifling air.

As the shots' reverberations faded away, the Trans Am descended the ramp and roared out toward I-30. Shortly, Bill was motoring west on the wide interstate, the T-tops off, a Steppenwolf cassette playing at full volume. The sky was so blue, and Bill could feel the afternoon's heat radiating up from the landscape…

Slowly, like a dissolve in the movies, the Trans Am's leather bucket seat became a luxurious desk chair, the steering wheel a computer mouse, and the music a ringing phone. The wide-open view of the Texas prairie became a vista of Wall Street office buildings from thirty stories up.

The man blinked a couple of times, regained his composure, then grabbed the phone. "Bill Estes."

"Mr. Estes, Mr. O'Connor's here to see you," his assistant announced. He could see her blurry shape through the sand-blasted glass office door. "Mr. Estes?"

"Sorry, Elaine, I was distracted. Who did you say it was?" Keyboards clacked in the background.

Elaine Cardoza, with Estes & Folderbrook for fifteen years, knew the particulars of all the firm's problem trades. "Mr. O'Connor. He owes the company over twenty million on that oil trade for delivery at the Marshall storage facility."

"I was expecting him. He can't pay."

"He must be here to ask for another delay."

"Probably. The monthly interest on the missed payment is $350,000." Bill hesitated for a moment. "Did you know Mr. O'Connor was an old friend of mine?"

"Yes, sir, I know you were in business together at one time."

Ms. Cardoza would not have recognized the cold, determined expression on the face of her employer. "Well, Mr. O'Connor pays today, or we put him into bankruptcy." Softly, Bill added, "It's time him and me split up."

Who I Would Become

by Michael Farrell

I slumped into an empty bench in the park, trying to enjoy the bright sun and the fresh air. It was an impromptu visit on my day off in an attempt to calm my racing mind.

Relax, Marty. It's your day off. You don't have to worry about the future.

Heck, all I could think about was the future. Once I finally moved out of my parents' place, my life became a constant string of deadlines, struggling to make ends meet while tackling all new responsibilities. I've been to this park hundreds of times since I was a kid, and yet I've never felt so lost.

Calm down, Marty. Just take in the scenery.

This park had seen better days. Dry patches of grass were scattered about. Fence posts, restrooms, and drinking fountains showed their age, as they either had broken sections or were wrought with corrosion and rust. I certainly remembered it being better during my childhood, but I knew it would never return to its former beauty. Despite many, many emails written to the local legislators, nobody wanted to invest back into the park. At the very least, the spring gave the oak trees a vibrant canopy of leaves with which to provide ample shade over the benches.

As I scanned the park, my eyes settled onto a silver Honda Civic pulling into a parking space. It reminded me of my mother's car with the bright sheen of the paint. The body of her car was always washed and waxed regularly, and I could spot that shiny paint in particular from a parking lot full of cars. Then again, I suppose Mom's not the only one who took

Collection 16

pride in her vehicles, and it can't be too unusual to see the same make and model on the road.

As I watched the car shut off, the rear door opened, and a young boy jumped out holding a soccer ball. I remembered playing soccer as a kid, too. It had its high and low points, but at least I got a trophy out of it to place on my dresser.

Something about that kid felt too familiar. A thought crossed my mind, but I dismissed it as something silly.

Maybe my brain is just throwing me for a loop. Just take a load off and relax.

After zoning out for a little bit, staring at the clouds, something tapped my foot. It was a soccer ball that stopped right between my feet. I picked up the ball, and as I sat up I saw the boy from earlier standing in front of me.

"Sorry," he said. He looked upset, probably expecting me to be annoyed.

At this close distance, I couldn't help but notice it. He looked exactly like me. At least, what I remembered looking like fifteen years ago. Same pale skin, same brown hair, same face, same body type—same everything. The only notable difference was an abundance of freckles on his cheeks, which I recalled having when I was younger until they went away with age. He *looked* like me, but he couldn't actually *be* me, could he?

I snapped myself out of my internal ramblings to break the awkward silence. "Oh, it's no problem, really." I handed the boy his ball. "What's your name, kid?"

"Marty," he said sheepishly, glancing at the soccer ball and refraining from eye contact.

Marty's a common name, right? The odds of a kid who looks like you and has your name can't be impossible, right?

I had to do something to get rid of this uncanny feeling.

I'll ask a question only I'll know. If he answers differently, I can brush this off as a weird coincidence. But what should I ask?

I cleared my throat and slouched forward, clasping my hands, and placing my elbows on my knees. "You, uh, play soccer in school, Marty?"

The boy nodded. "Yeah."

"So . . . how did that start?"

"It was my mom's idea," he said, ever so bluntly.

"You didn't want to do it though, right?"

The kid tilted his head. "How did you know that?"

"Oh, uh, it's a common situation." *Bah, that was too vague. Think, Marty. Think!* "Do you think you're good at it?"

He lowered his head. "No. I suck. I can't get the ball to go where I want it to."

At that moment, I remembered an event that only I could know about. *It's worth a shot. I have to know.*

I sat against the back of the bench, hands still clasped, trying to speak as gently as possible. "Have you ever . . . kicked the ball somewhere you really shouldn't have? Like . . . a window?"

Fear plastered the kid's face. His posture swayed as he fiddled with the soccer ball.

That's a nervous tick Mom used to call to my attention.

"It's fine," I said, trying to assure him. "I won't judge you. I've done stuff like that before."

"Yeah . . ." he said, struggling to utter that word loud enough to be heard.

Shame quickly washed over me. I remembered that event clearly. I was practicing at a friend's house when my friend went inside. As I practiced, I kicked the ball way harder than I should have. Once I heard the shattering of glass, I bolted back to my house. I was wrought with guilt for the next few weeks, afraid of being confronted and thinking that, try as I might, I would never be good at soccer. Just a screw-up of a person who could never improve. All those emotions and memories came back to me. I felt the same way this kid did, because this kid *was* me.

I need to apologize. This is no way to treat myself—or any kid. Gosh, I'm an idiot!

I slid over on the bench and gestured to the open space. Little Marty sat down, reluctantly, and set his soccer ball next to him.

"Hey, I'm sorry," I began, "I didn't mean to make you feel that way. I did the same thing when I was younger. It's hard to fess up to something like that. But I know what you can do to feel better."

He perked up his head. "You do?"

"The next thing you have to do is tell your mother about it."

"I don't want to! She'll be mad!"

"Yes, she will, because it was a dumb thing to do. But she'll help you, too. I know you find it hard to seek out help from others, and you're scared that they won't understand how you feel. But if you do this, you can let go of the guilt, and you'll get better at soccer."

"I can't get better at soccer."

"You may feel that way now, but you'll make some good memories doing it and look back on them later. What if I told you that, if you keep practicing, you'll go on to make a game-winning kick? You'll even get a trophy!"

Little Marty's eyes widened. "You think I will?"

"I know you will. You may feel like you're not capable, but you'll make mistakes, learn from them, and they'll become easier to do. Things can get better. You won't have the same problems forever."

Saying those words felt comforting to me. And my younger self felt the same. He straightened his posture and relaxed his shoulders.

I rose to my feet and let out a deep sigh. "Well, I've kept you long enough. You should go find your mother."

Little Marty grabbed his soccer ball and walked away. I began my walk back home in the other direction. *I think I've had enough of whatever's going on here.*

After that day, I would visit the park whenever I could in the event I'd see my younger self again. I never saw him again, but it was something I thought about often. However, throughout my repeated visits to the park, workers would come in and renovate the park's amenities, and landscapers would sod and maintain the grass. The park was like new. I guess all those complaints finally got through.

That day made me see how far I've come from the past, and how much I'm capable of improving in the future. And so, on one of my days off, I would find a bench and sit, imagining myself meeting my future self this time, and getting excited about who I would become next.

Becoming

by Jim R. Garrison

Antonio lay on his back in a thick stand of tall grass. Trees towered around him. A warm breeze wafted across his naked body.

Where am I? What is this place? How did I get here?

It was dark beneath a sky filled with stars, but he could see every detail around him as if it were the middle of the day.

How is this even possible?

Excruciating pain rippled through his body to his very marrow.

What's happening to me?

Earlier he and Cassandra lay together in his bedroom, entangled in unyielding rapture. Her vibrant red lips caressed his neck while her pale, soft skin pressed against him. Auburn hair formed a fiery halo surrounding Cassandra's oval face. She was the most beautiful woman he'd ever known, and she wanted him. What sane man could have refused her?

His entire body changed from the inside out, muscles growing more powerful. The pain was horrible yet delicious as his old body transitioned into something else, something different.

Antonio sat up and surveyed his surroundings, acutely aware of the tiniest details. He could hear the grass growing and insects chattering. He could hear every sound in the forest.

Somewhere near, he picked up the sounds of animals, and as if by some ancient instinct, he ran toward that sound faster than he ever thought was possible. Instantly he was upon a herd of deer and caught one of the larger animals. Confronting his prey, his mouth changed, incisors extended and became fangs, and he buried them in the animal's throat, draining that wonderful sweet substance. Renewed strength surged through his body. His hunger quenched, he tossed the dead animal and examined his surroundings.

Collection 16

A dirt road led from the forest. He followed it at a fast pace and soon came to a cabin set back from the road. He climbed the steps to the porch and struck the door with such force that it splintered and broke apart, held only by one unrelenting hinge.

Startled awake by the sudden intrusion, a large, bearded man threw back the bed covers and fumbled for a pistol that lay on the side table. He fired at the dark shape standing in the open doorway. Antonio avoided the bullet as if it were coming at him in slow motion.

With lightning speed, Antonio attacked the man with bone-crushing strength and buried his fangs in the man's neck. The man kicked and screamed, but any resistance quickly ceased as the blood drained from his body.

Letting the lifeless body fall to the floor, he stared at it for several breaths. He wiped his mouth with the back of his hand. *What have I done? What did I just do?*

He shook his head in disbelief, then gathered the man's clothing from a near-by chair and pulled on the jeans and T-shirt. A set of keys hung from a nail next to the smashed door. Barefoot, Antonio pocketed the keys on his way out of the cabin. He never looked back at the lifeless shell that lay crumpled on the floor. He got behind the wheel of the old red truck and began driving.

Turning onto a familiar highway, he accelerated. Lights appeared on the horizon as he neared the city. Several minutes later, he pulled into the driveway of his small brick ranch-style house.

The eastern horizon grew lighter. A flash of early morning sun singed his exposed neck. On the small stoop, he reached for the doorknob, but it opened on its own accord. As the first painful rays of light burned his back, a delicate yet powerful hand reached out and jerked him into the darkness of the room. The door slammed shut behind him.

"Cassandra?"

She had covered the windows so no sunlight could get through. Cassandra's body glowed with a phantom light from within. Her face was radiant with high cheekbones, almond-shaped glowing green eyes, and that mischievous smile.

"What did you do to me?" he demanded.

"How do you feel, Antonio? You look as if you've already feasted."

"I don't understand."

Her laugh was musical as she took his hands and pulled him against her. She kissed him, then backed away, studying his face, her eyes mesmerizing.

Metamorphosis

He couldn't turn away. He couldn't resist. Her thoughts came into his head, but they made no sense.

She kissed him again, and it was even more delicious. He never wanted to stop and was disappointed when she backed away again.

"You didn't answer me, Antonio. How do you feel?"

"I can't explain it. I feel different." He reached out for her, but she held him at arm's length.

"You are different, Antonio. I should explain."

"You're a vampire, aren't you?"

"Well, that's obvious." She smiled.

"You could have killed me, but you didn't. Why did you let me live?"

"That was never an option. I have searched for years to find a suitable mate. When we met, I knew you were an exceptional creature worthy to be with me."

"Creature?"

She grinned. "I meant to say 'human.'"

"I awoke in the woods and was all alone. I slaughtered a deer with my bare hands. I killed a man."

"I had to leave you there to make the transition. The change. The metamorphosis into what you are becoming. What I made you."

"For the first time in my life, I feel alive. What is happening to me? What did you do?"

"Now that you've had your fill of human blood, your body is changed. What you are now is only the beginning of what you will become. As you continue to feed, you will change even more until the transition is complete. You are no longer human, Antonio. What you once were is gone forever."

"I should hate you for what you've done."

She smiled and asked, "Do you, Antonio? Do you hate me?"

He shook his head. "No ... Maybe someday I will ... but not today."

Cassandra's thin gown fell from her shoulders, revealing a perfect porcelain body that shimmered in the darkened room. She smiled and held out her arms to him. Antonio ripped off his own clothing and came into her embrace. She pressed her ice-cold body against his; her sweet lips on his neck no longer seeking his blood.

They came together with such force and ecstasy that no human could have imagined or endured.

I'm Different

by Tilly Grey

Until he started public school and rode a special school bus, I don't think Norm knew he was different. His moment of truth came when he was eight. He had just started riding a bus that served not only children going to his special-needs program, but others who attended a school for the physically disabled. Only fifteen kids rode the small van, and one of them was a little girl whose legs were encased in braces. Like everything else about Norm, he was right out front about his feelings for this little girl.

"I love her. Want flower," he said. So, I wrapped the dripping stem of a daisy in a bit of foil, and Norm proudly climbed the bus with a flower for his new love. Soon it was pieces of candy or cookies, and for a couple of weeks he awoke each morning to the tremendous joy of riding the school bus with someone he loved and who seemed to care for him as well.

Then came the morning I got a call from Norm's teacher.

"Something's terribly wrong," she said. "Norm's sitting under a table and won't come out. He's horribly upset."

I drove to Norm's school. When he saw me, he came out from under the table and threw himself into my arms crying.

"What's wrong? What's wrong?" I babbled.

"I'm different." He sobbed. "I'm different."

I looked at his teacher. She sighed and shook her head. Neither of us had expected this to happen so soon. I did the only thing I knew how to do: I sat down holding my son, my face buried in his hair, murmuring, "I love you. Dad loves you. Your sister Hilary loves you."

Of course, it didn't mean a thing because the little girl on the bus, who was not mentally disabled, had said something cruel to him; something that catapulted him from the secure world he had always known into some other alien place.

He was "different."

Some people say mentally challenged people don't feel things as deeply as "normal" people; that people with Down syndrome are happy and never feel hurt or angry. Wrong.

I drove Norm to and from school for the rest of that year. I hoped he would have recovered his sense of joy by the summer.

We spend our summers in a small house on a remote Maine island called Criehaven. We share the island with ten lobstermen and their families and one or two renters. No roads, no electricity, no stores, no phones; just multi-colored buoys rescued from rocks; strawberries, blueberries, raspberries, and blackberries; roses; seagulls, eider ducks, and puffins; lobsters, seals, dolphins, the occasional whale, and every kind of fish that lives in the ever-changing sea.

Ours is the only house at the eastern end of Criehaven—a mile from the harbor down a rocky path. But we have our garden, outhouse, outdoor fireplace, rain barrels for fresh water and a sun shower hanging from a tree. Inside we use propane gas for a few lights, the stove, and the refrigerator.

Norm loves the island because he is "normal" there. He can safely come and go from the house as he pleases. In fact, he often comes in and out the back door several times calling to me, "Going out, Mom."

Normally, he is up and down from the rocky beach, swimming with his sister, searching for buoys, or tossing rocks into the waves.

Normally, he loves walking down the narrow path to the harbor to pass the time with some of the lobstermen. The islanders know him and are more than kind.

That summer, however, he sat for hours, legs crossed in the lotus position, tossing rocks into the sea. When Hilary asked him to play tag, he replied, "No thanks."

It became clear he preferred to be alone. He had erected a protective shield around himself. I feared he was withdrawing from us as well as from a world he had learned could no longer be trusted.

Collection 16

One day, I came down to the beach and found Norm carefully drying out some damp school books he had recovered from a green garbage bag that had washed ashore. His new treasures looked like workbooks belonging to perhaps a first or second grader.

Fortunately, the child used a pencil to copy the names of flags, animals, flowers, and other objects so that the water, which had seeped into the garbage bag, effectively erased the words, leaving Norm with a set of workbooks that he christened "My Work."

He gathered up the dried books and put them in his special drawer, and every time his younger sister, Hilary, settled down to write—she had just started second grade—Norm went to his drawer, got out a workbook, and scribbled symbols under each of the pictured objects.

I knew what he was doing. He had schoolwork just like Hilary. Maybe if he did the same thing she did, he would not be different anymore.

Then one night, something wonderful happened.

In our funny little cabin, the children sleep on mattresses in a primitive loft. Because Norm is afraid of the dark, I keep a kerosene lamp—set inside a chicken wire cage nailed high upon a rafter—burning low.

This particular night, the lamp went out, and Norm woke up crying. I didn't feel like coping with the kerosene lantern at two in the morning, so I brought him down the ladder and put him in my bed in our living room that faces a bank of windows overlooking the sea. A lighted candle burned beside the bed. Norm fell asleep quickly, but when I blew out the candle, he awoke, sat up, gasped, and cried out, "Mom. Stars."

He insisted on going out onto our deck.

He obviously knew what stars were. He could identify them in a picture of Heaven in his Bible. But I don't think he knew where stars were before this night. His eyesight is poor and, in our light-heavy suburb, I doubt he'd ever seen them. But here, on a clear, moonless night, on a dark island, it was different. The sky was brilliant with glowing spheres, sparkling, and flickering.

Hilary woke up and came down from the loft, and when she saw how excited Norm was, she insisted we pull our sleeping bags outside onto the deck. We lay there watching Norm point to one twinkling orb after another and clapping his hands. There was red Mars glowing to the east, and the stars of the summer triangle, Vega, Deneb, and Altair,

Metamorphosis

shining down on us. Plus, all the other stars which I couldn't name. But it didn't matter to Norm. He loved them all.

The next day, my son kept saying, "'Member the stars, Mom?" And as soon as it began to get dark, he ran out onto the deck to check that they were back. As they appeared out of the dusk, he raised his arms and began a stumbling dance accompanied by a tuneless song.

Once again, we all slept on the deck and watched the stars.

The following morning, Hilary said to me, "Norm's acting funny. He told me he was going to find water."

"Probably just going to the beach."

"No, Mom. He said it in a complete sentence."

I rushed out the door and saw Norm walking down the path to the beach. But he was walking straight: no lunging gait and he even looked taller.

I followed him to the beach. He was digging in the sand with a piece of driftwood.

"There is sweet water here," he said: a complete sentence. And, just then, water filled up the hole he was digging. He scooped up a handful and drank. "It's good." He smiled at me. "Now we will always have fresh water."

Then he stood up and began skipping rocks into the waves rolling onto the shore. Just like a normal boy.

Every day when I wake up now, I wonder what Norm will be like this morning. There are days I find myself fondly remembering him the way he was before.

The only thing I know now for sure is that when he comes down for breakfast he will be different.

Dirtball

by John Hope

I can't think of a more boring place in the world than my twin brother's football game. Eleven-year-old boys padded and helmeted bounce and roll over each other out on the field. Though Hudson and I are twins—fraternal twins—we're so different that most people don't realize we're brothers.

He's tall. I'm short.
He's got muscles. I've got bones.
He loves football. I like Monopoly.
He's Cool Hudson. I'm Peewee the Nerd.
And right now, I'm stuck up here on these metal bleachers. Bubblegum-chewing moms and nose-picking little sisters surround me on all sides.
"Sack 'em! Sack 'em, Noah!" Mom yells.
I wince.
Near the field, little girls wear bright-blue skirts and wave pompoms in sync with a staticky song screeching through overhead speakers. The droning voice of an old man calls out stuff about the game from a bullhorn. At the far end, a scoreboard with the bright numbers of a clock clicking down reminds me how stupidly long this game is.
I tug on Mom's sleeve. "Mom?"
"What, Peewee?" She sounds annoyed.
I ask, "Is it the last quarter?"
"No. It's only the second quarter."
"How many quarters are there?"
"Four. You know that."
I groan. This game is forever. I look up to see a pair of girls munch on long ropes of red licorice, my favorite candy. My mouth waters.

Metamorphosis

"Mom?" I bounce.

"What, Peewee? I'm busy." She looks away. "Get that boy! Get him!"

"Can I have some licorice? Please?"

She doesn't answer.

"Mom? Mom?"

"Ooo!" She bangs a fist into her leg. "I could wring that ref's neck right now!"

I gulp.

Deciding not to get killed, I ease away from her. At the end of our bench, I limbo under a handrail and jump down onto the dirt below. Distant whistles, gleeful cheerleaders, and the squeaking clangs of footsteps on the bleachers merge like mixing corn and mashed potatoes together on a dinner plate.

I dart to the concession stand. There, two little boys wave a dollar bill at a wrinkled old lady behind the counter. She fetches a couple sticks of red licorice from a glass jar, and the two take their prize. They stroll past me with their long, red treats swaying from their mouths like tails.

I lick my lips and wish I had money. Defeated, I sulk away, hands in my pocket.

Cheers from the bleachers, yells from the cheerleaders, barks from the coaches, and huffs from the boys playing football all remind me how much I'd rather be playing Minecraft at home right now.

I turn away from it all and walk toward the back of the bleachers. I hear a different sound—the arguing of boys.

Seven shirtless boys, all about my age, gather just behind the bleachers. Two taller boys—one skinny, one fat—point from head to head counting aloud.

"But that's not even," the skinny one says. "Your team has more."

The fat one says, "Well, then . . ." He spins. "Hey you, kid."

I point to myself. "Me?"

"Yeah. C'mere."

I near and, before I can complain, I'm whisked into their game. They divide up. I'm shoveled toward one end of their field, a strip of crabgrass and weeds between the back of the bleachers and a chain-linked fence.

"Kick off!" someone shouts.

The opposite team chucks a dark object into the air toward our end. I realize it's a cup of dirt pinched into a ball. It sails through the air,

Collection 16

spins, and tosses a beautiful spray of dirt like water from a sprinkler. My team races forward. One catches the cup. An explosion of dirt rains over everyone, me included. I swallow and taste the bitter earth on my tongue. Boys slam into each other. I'm hit. I smash to the ground and roll.

"Line it up!" someone calls.

I stand, lightheaded.

The other boys are already lining up—my team on one side and the other team facing them. The tall kids wrinkle their noses at me as if annoyed that I'm taking too long.

I bounce up and line up with the rest.

"Hike!"

The boys push and maneuver around each other.

I get shoved to the ground, and I roll. Kids continue racing around me as I sit up. My shirt is filled with as much dirt as the cup of dirt we're using for a football.

"Interception!"

The fat boy on the other team jumps up with the cup of dirt in his grip.

The skinny boy says, "Hey. You were tackled."

The fat boy says, "Yeah. But not before I intercepted your pass, idiot."

"Line it up!"

I jump to my feet, yank off my shirt, and line up with the rest of my team.

"Hike!"

I try to get past the boy ahead of me to chase after the fat boy with the cup of dirt. A boy knocks me over. I hit the dirt. Something hits me in the gut.

I gasp.

Once I find my breath, I notice the fat boy lying face down on the ground next to me. The cup of dirt is loose on the ground. I scramble to my feet, grab the cup, and race toward the other end of the field. I hear shouts from behind. I run at top speed. Footsteps approach. I reach the end. A body slams onto my back. I stumble but then lift from the ground, my feet dangling.

I look down. My feet dangle. The skinny boy swings me through the air in celebration. The rest of my team cheers as rain falls on us, changing the dirt into mud. The big boy drops me, and I high-five others as the rain grows heavy.

Metamorphosis

"Peewee!"

I wipe rain from my face to see Mom standing at the other end of our field, holding a piece of paper above her head to block the rain. "Peewee!" She waves at me to follow her.

I give the boys a goodbye smile and take off toward Mom, grabbing my muddy shirt along the way.

The rain is blasting us by the time we get to Mom's van. Inside, Hudson and I sit on the bench behind the drivers' seat where Mom sits. She winces at us. "You two are filthy." She starts the car.

Hudson wiggles out of his shoulder pads and then stares at me—shirtless and muddy. He gnaws on the side of his plastic mouthguard as if it were red licorice. "How'd cha' get so dirty?"

"Dirtball."

"Dirtball?"

I nod. "Some boys filled a paper cup with dirt, and we played football with it."

A smile creeps up his face. "That's cool." He holds out a fist.

I bump it with my fist.

He looks out the window still gnawing on his mouthguard.

I lean back, smile, and crunch grains of dirt between my teeth. I taste the lovely grossness and decide I like it better than red licorice. My feet tap against Hudson's muddy shoulder pads. I wonder what it'd be like wearing them and playing real football. Never in my life had I considered playing a sport or competing in anything that didn't involve a video controller or dice. But now, as I roll my tongue, I consider maybe a little taste of dirt is all it takes to transform Peewee the Nerd into a kid like Hudson.

Freaky Thursday

by **Kelly Karsner-Clarke**

I am with Lauren the day she jots down her 9,843,242,567th story idea. This one is about the ghost of a character coming back to haunt an author after being "killed" in revisions.

Lauren loved writing. Being an author is her dream. But she'll never open that Google doc again.

Lauren dies the next Thursday. I am with her then too. She's driving to work when a drunk guy in a Mack Truck comes barreling out of nowhere. She is too young, and it is a horrible and senseless tragedy.

Too bad nobody else knows she's dead.

Here is what I do remember of that day.

It's not that Lauren goes into the light, but more that she gets sucked up by the big vacuum of mortality. I watch from her shadow while she's reunited with her little brother Danny; I feel all her joy and grief for the what-could-have-been for both of them.

Danny listens while Lauren completely freaks out. How can their parents get through losing yet another child in yet another highway accident? It will destroy them! And Lauren's kids are little—they need her.

As Lauren rails on, strangely familiar ghosts collect around her. It takes me a while to place them. They're characters Lauren wrote in her stories; stories in various stages of waiting to be polished and submitted.

But I'll let you in on a little secret: the Great Author of the Universe makes and trashes Her rough drafts too.

I'm an early character sketch of Lauren, discarded in rewrites. Lauren is prettier, smarter, gets stuff done better, more empathetic . . . also more likeable, believable, and relatable. I'll never understand how I didn't just stay in the Author's trash folder. Maybe the Author Herself doesn't know.

"It's not your time," Danny tells Lauren. "You need to go back now."

"You tell her! She has to finish my story." The morally gray, toilet-dwelling glitter demon antagonist of Lauren's favorite manuscript smirks.

"Just a minute longer?" Lauren looks dazed. "I've missed you so much!"

Maybe it's the Author who thinks She's pushed Lauren back to Earth.

Maybe it's Danny.

Maybe Lauren accidentally pushes me instead of jumping herself. The one bad thing I can say about her is that she was too nice, naively assuming she could make anyone into their best self.

Whatever happens, Lauren doesn't go back into her body.

I do.

I come to with a mouthful of broken glass and lawn growing through my car window. It feels like every cell in my body is giving birth with no epidural.

"Jesus, she's peeing glass shards," gripes a paramedic.

"I have to give the truck driver a ticket," scowls the highway patrol officer. "It's the skid marks on the road; the eyewitnesses . . ."

Why does he sound angry?

It turns out the Mack Truck driver likes to make up stories too. Before I can remember how to spell Lauren's name, he's the community's new literary darling with a brand-new story featuring yours truly as the monster.

It's hard for me to speak now, and a lot of people don't believe me about the accident anyway. Maybe they do explain why beyond, "Nobody survives that!" But it's hard for me to understand what people are saying now too.

So, I don't even try to tell anybody I'm actually not Lauren.

The year Lauren was in fourth grade, she checked Mary Rodgers's *Freaky Friday* out of the school library three times in two months. She'd sit on her saucer chair, under the carousel horses her mom had stenciled on her wall, and read.

I'm not as confused in Lauren's body as Rodgers's character Annabel is in her mom's. All I remember are some of Lauren's memories. Except I remember them happening to me. We have the exact same feelings about all of them.

If I were writing a story about how my memory works, someone in Lauren's critique group would tell me that disability makes no logical sense. But the illogical is my reality.

Some days, I can remember entire passages of books that Lauren hasn't read in twenty-five-plus years.

Collection 16

But then I *can't* remember: Where Lauren's house is. What someone said three seconds ago. What other people's faces look like. And on. And on. And on.

Some days I struggle to speak, forget simple words, or say dumb things.

One day I tell Lauren's son (my son?) to take an oven because his feet stink. He heads to the bathroom, laughing hysterically.

Other people aren't as understanding.

Now that I have speech disabilities, people often tell me I have always been overly opinionated, too snarky, think I'm funny when I'm really not. Weird, I remember many of them always telling Lauren they loved how she was decisive and witty.

Lauren was great at typing, punctuation, math . . . but I'm trying to figure them out with a billion new learning disabilities that I've never heard of.

People are sympathetic for a week or two. Then they get fed up . . . "Grow up and get your crap together. You went to freaking Georgetown!"

Did I though? I remember Lauren's time there as well as if it had been my own. But Lauren got a *B+* in Econometrics, and I can't add into the double digits.

The processes I pick up the fastest are the rules of story writing. I'm somehow a good writer too and need those fictional worlds to escape into more than ever.

Maybe writing is my redemption?

Nah.

Seeing that I can write well almost makes people even angrier that my math, memory, and auditory processing all suck.

Maybe they just want Lauren back. Hey, *I* want Lauren back, even if it means I'd evaporate.

But I'm not sure how well most people really knew Lauren. They didn't realize how much she loved writing and hated her corporate job. I think it's partly she didn't tell them and partly they didn't listen.

So many people say my acquired disabilities prove that I'm "bad." But how can that be true when I share one of my biggest loves with Lauren and even the Great Author Herself?

I submit Lauren's glitter demon story to the Rising Kite contest at an SCBWI conference.

Honorable Mention!

Metamorphosis

Somehow, my new boss finds out. "You have time to write freaking children's books, but you can't even make an effort to walk, stay awake, listen, or be organized!"

Like too many people, he heard the truck driver's story first and thinks I'm either crazy or faking.

But one day, a coworker pulls me aside. "I believe you about your brain injury. My aunt's friend is an attorney. She can help you." And she AirDrops me a number.

My coworker is the deus ex machina who has incited her another rewrite. One that adds a lot more chapters to the rest of my life.

The attorney comes barreling in. There is a lot of money and ego on the line in any personal injury case, and it seems like every week she uncovers yet another bad actor.

But she has a path to clean up the ugly mess.

She sends me to a big shot neurologist.

So many pills.

So many shots.

So many sessions with the speech therapist.

So many fights about the transcription device that allows me to participate in conversations again.

I'll need all of it for the rest of my life.

But these new supporting characters make me much sharper than I used to be.

"You don't heal from traumatic brain injury," the neurologist tells me a few thousand times. "You learn to live with your symptoms."

The green pills make me constantly sick to my stomach. But they keep me from falling into the defense attorney's mind games in deposition.

He confronts me with the out-there and incredibly disturbing stories the truck driver's camp has spun up about me. Laid out in a line like that, they're packed with logical inconsistencies and plot holes . . . all written up in affidavit.

"You only won that Rising Kite contest because people pity you and your so-called disabilities," is the defense attorney's parting shot.

Deposition is not the time to tell him the Rising Kite contest is anonymous.

Lauren was an amazing writer. I miss her so much.

But I'm grateful she left me with the tools to create my own amazing stories.

A Change of Heart
by Michele Verbitski Knudsen

As Alex Zell's assistant, I got an apartment tucked into the back corner of the billionaire's penthouse on Park Avenue. Big deal, he demoted me from partner to personal assistant the minute his father died. Nice son, huh? My loving son had changed.

Standing in the rooftop garden enjoying the spicy-sweet fragrance of floribunda roses with Manhattan's glittering lights against an indigo sky, I waited for the cleaners to finish. While they eliminated the stench of cigars, cigarettes, and booze from the patterned Orientals and modern white-on-white sectionals, I worried about Alex's health and his lavish all-night parties.

The distant blaring horns and screaming sirens increased as dawn approached. With everything scrubbed and deodorized, I sought the solace of my bed.

As I entered my apartment, the intercom blasted.

"Elenor!" Alex's coughing and gagging filled the air. "Come . . ."

Calling me Elenor also began when his father died. I dashed to Alex's bedroom. Flinging open the door, I found blood splatters—everywhere. Splotches of red dotted the white bedding and carpet, and a smeared handprint sullied the wall from his second episode this month.

Across the room, a brunette stood naked, her trembling hands attempting to cover herself. Grabbing a towel, I went to her. "Here, dear. Looks worse than it is. Capillaries in Mr. Zell's esophagus rupture when a coughing fit occurs. Scary, but it ends quickly. He'll be fine." I led her to the guest bathroom, retrieving her belongings along the way. "You can wash up here, then go through the door at the end. Our driver will take you home."

Metamorphosis

I guided Alex to his ensuite; his arm cold and clammy in my grip. "Calm yourself. Take short breaths. The coughing will subside once you relax."

Beads of sweat formed on his upper lip as blood dripped from his double chin and ran down his protruding stomach. I turned on the shower.

"Jenny?"

"All taken care of."

Alex nodded. "Won't see her again," he croaked.

At thirty-seven, I doubted he would ever find a wife. "Have a long soak in the whirlpool while I . . . tidy up."

I alerted our housekeeper and called the private number of our personal physician who agreed to an immediate house call. An hour later, Alex lay sound asleep in his pristine white bedroom.

The view from my office windows mesmerized me. Central Park appeared as a leafy-green rectangle surrounded by pale skyscrapers. A scream emanating from Alex's chrome-and-glass corner office shattered my serenity. I hurried over.

He pointed to the television. ". . . picketing *our* building—downstairs! Call the police." He cleared his throat. "Throw them in jail."

A dozen tenants carrying signs marched out front. I called our attorney and, on his advice, I invited the picketers in.

"Everyone's waiting in the conference room, Alex."

"Let them wait."

"Our lawyer said they can hold up construction, so try to be a *little* empathetic."

"Oh . . . all right."

The yellowish pallor of Alex's skin and his recent weight loss concerned me even though a month had passed without another episode. "Please, just listen. Getting upset might bring on another coughing spell."

Alex held up his hand, nodded, and we walked into the long beige room. Five men and women sat on each side of the glass-topped table with David and Loren Anderson at one end. David, a sandy-haired architect, designed city projects, and Loren, a vivacious blonde, worked as head scrub nurse at a local hospital.

Collection 16

"Good morning. Mr. Zell wants to hear your ideas."

Alex gestured toward the spokespeople. "Mr. or Mrs. Anderson?"

Loren Anderson stood. "You've earned millions turning rental units into high-priced condominiums—throwing your tenants out in the street."

"Here, here," yelled a man on the right.

"Hampton Place renters want you to sell us our apartments *as is* at an affordable price. You wouldn't make your usual killing, but you'd earn the community's goodwill."

David rose. "We all agree with Loren, but I realize you're in business to make money." He handed Alex some plans. "These buildings in the Bronx are selling at give-away prices. Buy them, remodel, then Hampton Place renters and other displaced people could afford to live there. Revitalizing the neighborhood and securing homes for thousands could be your legacy."

David sat, and Loren brushed a lock of his hair from his forehead and winked.

"I'll take your suggestions under advisement." Alex walked out.

For the next six months, Alex continued to drink, smoke, and party even after two stents. He believed money could fix anything until a major heart attack struck—nearly killing him.

Shortness of breath and weakness from his damaged heart plus uncontrollable bleeding from cirrhosis caught up with him. Sitting in a hospital bed, oxygen hissing up his nose, Alex couldn't fathom how his twenty-million-dollar gift failed to propel him to the top of the waiting list for organ donors.

Between the drugs and lack of oxygen, Alex appeared confused. "Can't you find a willing *foreign* donor?"

"Willing? If anyone gave you their heart and liver, they'd be dead. Your doctors agreed a partial liver wouldn't work in your case and as for your heart—"

"But . . ." Coughing ensued with blood.

The nurse rushed to him. Feeling helpless, I slipped out and headed for the cafeteria.

Metamorphosis

In the dining room, I passed Loren Anderson. She sat staring into her coffee as tears trickled down her cheeks. She appeared thinner than I remembered.

Going through the line, I snagged meatloaf dinners and iced tea for two and carried them to her table. "May I join you?"

Loren wiped her tears, produced a weak smile, and nodded. She didn't object when I placed the steaming meal in front of her. I hoped the savory aroma would entice her to eat.

"Please, join me."

She picked up her fork and ate mechanically until her plate was empty. "Thank you, Mrs. Zelenofski."

"Elenor, please."

Loren smiled. "Elenor."

"Visiting a friend or relative?"

Her chin quivered.

"I'm so sorry . . . didn't mean to pry."

"My David . . . bad car accident. He's . . . on life support . . . brain dead. Doctors keep pressuring me to pull the plug, but . . . he's all I've got. Next week, I won't even have a place to live."

Thanks to my son.

Another of Alex's countless casualties—pushed out of Manhattan by sky-rocketing prices and greedy businessmen. While he lay dying, Alex spoke of halting the Hampton Place project, but it was too late. My mind came up with the perfect solution, if special criteria could be met.

I needed to help my son, and Loren Anderson needed a home. When blood and tissue typing revealed that Alex and David proved to be a good match, I suggested some conditions Loren should insist on.

Armed with legal papers, Loren marched into Alex's hospital room. Ten minutes later, she came out with a signed agreement in hand. The medical procedures commenced.

At my insistence, Loren moved into the guest suite in our penthouse while her apartment underwent renovation. When the hospital released Alex, Loren offered help with his rehab and spent her days encouraging him, making him laugh, and seeing he stuck to doctor's orders.

Collection 16

As he regained strength, I noted a distinct change in his attitude. He no longer yelled or lost his temper. It seemed obvious Alex sought Loren's approval as his pale-blue eyes followed her every move.

In the months that followed, they visited galleries and museums along with homeless shelters and old buildings in the other boroughs. I sometimes caught them whispering or holding hands.

With letters for Alex to sign, I padded into his office and caught them kissing.

"Mother!" Alex cried.

That word brought joy to my soul. I hadn't heard it in years. "Sorry."

Alex laughed. "Stay, please." He handed me a folder. "These are plans David designed for those buildings in the Bronx. Let's get started on them."

"Fabulous." My son finally decided to do good things with his money.

Alex put his arms around Loren. "This lovely lady has agreed to marry me."

Loren brushed a lock of his hair from his forehead and smiled.

"Congratulations!" I hugged them both.

I didn't know whether his near-death experience, organs from a better man, or the love of a kind and generous woman brought about this metamorphosis. It didn't matter, I got my loving son back.

"Loren," Alex called, already down the hall.

"Coming David . . . um . . . Alex." She winked at me and ran to him.

Waterbags

by **Anthony Malone**

We stood naked in a straight line and filed into the courtroom. Stopping in front of the bench, we stood at attention as disciplined soldiers might. Various body types, ages, heights, shapes, and skin tones, we were a smorgasbord of humanity. A court official, draped in his robe of office, was at the column's end.

"Face the Magistrate!" We made a methodical, painful turn. The Magistrate loomed behind a large mahogany desk, his throne of authority, high above eye level. I strained my neck to see his face. Our subservient position reminded us of who was in control as he peered down at us with bored omniscience.

"Are you foolish enough to think we don't know your most intimate secrets? Your secrets are known to all, as is your malfeasance."

We looked down at our feet to hide our shame. Finality and defeat sucked away the remainder of our strength. Some wept.

My inner voice screamed, "We are now your obedient prisoners. That's what you wanted to hear, isn't it? When will this end?"

The gallery behind us was sparsely occupied with visitors. My soulmate was there. Her pain and uncertainty added to my discomfort. We'd been together forever! As an outsider to these proceedings, many unanswered questions filled her thoughts, but she dared not formulate them for fear of being scolded or ejected from the process. Out of her realm, she only could observe my suffering as I observed her torment. I realized the only reason she had permission to be here was that it added to my punishment.

The Magistrate's gavel smacked three sharp cracks, sounding like a bullwhip.

Collection 16

"Attention! Attention! We are here for judgment and sentencing."

"Yes, Magistrate."

"I declare this process in motion and within the guidelines of the Fourth Realm."

He waved his arm. A large mirror, wide enough to encompass reflections of all internees, appeared behind us.

"Now. Everyone, turn around and look into the mirror."

"Yes, Magistrate."

We turned in small increments and did an about-face. Our bodies felt like they weighed a thousand pounds each. Our hands and feet, bricks. We perspired profusely just from the physical act of turning. Fat beads of sweat slid off our wet, shiny skin and fell to the floor. The droplets tapped an erratic beat on the hard tile.

There was a minute's pause as we struggled to turn. Only the shuffling of bare feet could be heard. Sagging flesh jiggled like bags of water. Everyone turned and settled to peer into the mirror. First, there was silence. Then gasps ensued followed by desperate, forlorn wailing.

"What have you done to us—elitist scum!"

"Now, now, Eighteen. That attitude has created your present predicament.

"All of you, observe yourselves in a new light, naked to the world. See what you look like and who you really are. Get a good look. Let it saturate your being, enter your soul."

His gavel slapped its pad three more times.

"Enough! Now, face the bench."

My body quivered; muscles tightened into knots. Could this be fear? I cringed at the force of his will.

"You are here for reckoning. A brief formality."

"Yes, Magistrate."

"After reviewing your histories, I have decided on the appropriate punishments. I feel they're fair and just."

"Yes, Magistrate."

"I will call your number. You will step forward to hear your sentence. Then you will step back in line so I can judge the next prisoner." A slight nod signaled the bailiff to begin reading from the scroll.

Metamorphosis

"After a thorough review of your cases, Magi has come to a reckoning." Bailiff scanned the line of detainees from left to right. "Prisoner Eighteen, step forward. Look up when Magi speaks."

The Magistrate's eyes fixed on me. "You will serve ninety-three years. Till death!"

"Yes, Mag—"

"Back in line, fool!" The bailiff roughly forced me into my place.

"Prisoner Seventeen, step forward."

"Seventy-three years. Till death!"

"Prisoner Sixteen, fifty-five years. I would gladly give you twice more, but we do have laws to follow. Let me say you will suffer every one of those years. Till death!"

And so it continued down the line to the last soul.

His gavel rapped three more times—three gunshots. The gallery flinched.

"You will be confined in a prison so small that you'll scream and wail for forgiveness. Some will try and stop the pain by ending their own lives. This is not acceptable and will be dealt with harshly. You will enter this new world and join your fellow inmates, legions of walking dead, just as yourselves. Serving life sentences, just as yourselves. Born into purgatory to suffer, repent, and learn."

The bailiff stepped forward. "Magi, it is time."

Magistrate nodded in agreement. "Take them to the embarkation area. Assign them a birthing mother. Give the good-riddance speech, and send them on their way. Bring in the next group. Come right back. We have a full calendar."

"Of course, Magi."

"Prisoners, pay attention. "Right face. Follow me through the door."

Above the door, a sign in ornate-gold lettering read Embarkation/Birthing Room. We lined up once again and waited for instructions. But first came the speech.

"As ethereal beings, you have lived for millennia as pure thought. Never have you felt the confinement or weight of the human vessel that will now be your prison. The crushing weight and loneliness will destroy you or make you stronger. Your thoughts will be yours and yours alone and cannot be shared instantaneously. You will learn how to walk. How to talk. I tell you truly, it will be most unforgettable."

Collection 16

An attendant appeared from the side. "Sir, we are ready for embarkation."

All prisoners were back to their ethereal presence in the staging area. We were all elated to be shed of the disgusting waterbag-meat-sack bodies we were imprisoned in for sentencing. We relaxed and felt free again. Thankful to be back to our original essence.

That was the most horrible thing I've ever experienced, came a thought.

So glad that's over with, came a different thought.

A new appreciation of what we were had blossomed.

The bailiff looked up from his paperwork. "Sorry, we're just in the staging area."

"Prisoner Eighteen, we have located your birthing mother. Come forward, please."

"Birthing what? Aren't we done? I can't take any more of this. No more!"

"Eighteen. This outburst will be our little secret. You haven't even started. You're leaving now to slide through your mother's loins, to be born into a penal colony with all the other wretched souls: the walking dead."

"No. Oh no!"

The thought of being imprisoned again started me wailing and screaming.

"Perfect, Eighteen. Hold that thought. That's exactly what they should hear as you're forced down the birthing canal and squeezed out into your new life on Penal Colony Earth.

Sentenced, ninety-three years—till death! See you then."

Ghost Pirates

by Meredith Martin

Ghost stories were a tradition in our neighborhood when I was a kid. There was no TV, so our entertainment was listening to stories being told by the local expert storyteller: my older brother, Bud. The gang, consisting of eight or nine kids between the ages of ten and twelve, would gather in our backyard on dark nights lighted by a shimmering shrouded moon. We would sit around a small, crackling campfire as Bud regaled us with haunting tales so vivid we would quiver with terror. He would drop his voice to a hoarse whisper, acquiring the tonelessness of a zombie. It would seem to enfold us like a sinister cloak and draw us into his whirling, spinning cosmos of fantasy. We were simultaneously thrilled and terrified.

One of my favorite tales was of the one-armed pirate, Gar. This scruffy, raggedy ghost is said to haunt Fort Island in Homosassa, Florida, where rumor has it that he lost an arm defending his ill-gotten gold. He replaced his lost appendage with a beautiful but savage glistening golden hook. He buried the rest of his gold on the island where he continues to guard it to this day.

It is told that on the nights when the moon is full, exactly at the stroke of midnight, for a brief fifteen minutes, the gold rises to the surface of the sand and glimmers in the moonlight, twinkling like stars, before receding again deep into the sand.

Many a treasure hunter sought their fortune when the full moon shone on the watery, forbidding island. They returned with strange tales of glittering spots appearing on the sand at the stroke of midnight. But when they approached the spot, it would move deeper into the island luring them farther into the desolate mangroves. As they followed it, they began to get the eerie feeling that something or someone was watching them. A whisper in the palms or a soft footstep behind soon destroyed their resolve, whereupon they quickly turned around and hightailed it back to their cars. They returned with empty pockets and a firm conviction of having seen Gar. Some felt the icy cold of his hook on their necks.

So, when Halloween arrived and my three teenage boys began to moan and groan that they were too old for Halloween . . . it was just boring fantasy anyway; I thought, *Oh Yeah—not this year. The moon is full, and we are going to Fort Island in search of gold!*

The kids knew the legend and jumped at the chance. At 11:30 we piled into my Jeep Cherokee and headed off to find our treasure. The road to Fort Island was a narrow two lane that twisted and turned through the uninhabited mangrove marsh like a four-mile-long, hideous snake ready to devour all trespassers. When we got to the island at 11:45, the huge jack-o'-lantern moon illuminated the silvery thread of beach. Dan, my oldest, handed out shovels, bags, and flashlights to his younger brothers—Pete and Frank. I led the way down the sandy path to the beach. We crouched in the sand, breathing shallowly, while listening to the night creatures call to each other. We peered into the night and dared not speak. At precisely midnight, a small light began to twinkle on the beach. It grew stronger. Then there was another. And another.

We let out a collective gasp and grabbed each other in a bear hug. As we began moving stealthily toward the twinkling patch, it suddenly moved closer to the dark, forbidding palms. We followed. It was uncanny. Each time we almost reached the patch, it would move again—deeper and deeper into the foliage. Then suddenly everything was as quiet as a tomb. My flashlight went out as did Pete's and Frank's. Only Dan's stayed lighted. The wind began to rustle the palm leaves which seemed to whisper, "Gar." I felt something hard and cold on my neck. I screamed; the boys dropped their shovels, and we all took off with Dan leading the way.

We tumbled into the car. I fumbled with the key before finally getting it into the ignition. The engine roared to life like a poked lion, and I tore out of the parking lot. My heart was hammering as I hugged the curves of the desolate road. I was driving like the hounds of the Baskerville family were on my tail. Nervously glancing in the rearview mirror, I could swear

I saw a ghastly apparition with grinning white teeth hanging onto my spare tire rack.

Once safely back home, we sputtered and shook, pulling each other into a group hug and grinning sheepishly. Pete said, "That was a cool Halloween, Mom."

"Yeah, like really . . . you're the best," echoed both Dan and Frank.

"Yeah," I said, "isn't it crazy how your imagination can run away with you like that? I have to admit that I was really scared, too."

As I walked around to the back of the Jeep, the hair on my neck rose when I saw a faint glitter of gold on my spare tire frame. Was Gar real? And if so, why were we not harmed and just frightened away? A smile played upon my mouth as I realized there really was a supernatural world that quietly existed alongside mine. Not a mean, vicious one— but rather one that would never hurt anyone. One that just wanted to participate and join in the fun of the story.

From Coffee Spill to Australia

by George August Meier

Even the most brilliant among us cannot say what changes await around the next blind corner.

He and the sports car—a ready accomplice—loved the speed. He ignored the obvious warning offered by the steam escaping the cup's lid. The sip. A scorched lip shot a pain-fueled hand away, the coffee cup striking leather-clad steering wheel. The lid flew. Liquid heat gushed over the rim onto hand and lap. Fingers on fire. With his left hand steering the ground rocket, the right holding the hot vessel, and lap heat increasing in intensity—he was position-trapped. Distress sanctioned a perversity—stain-containing cup heaved to the floor. The free hand lifted wet pants from groin. He let out a groan and sigh. A dark-blue blur from the left.

Loud, violent, intrusive steel. Chaos and crushing.

Darkness.

An undefined glow hangs in front of him like a translucent yellow curtain, yet his eyes are shut. There is a muffled beeping. He tries to assess. There is contact with the back of his head, shoulders, buttocks, and heals. *I must be lying down.*

He struggles to open his eyes but can't. He wants to call out but can't. His thought process is sluggish. It takes a while to consider moving an arm. *I can't do anything. Damn, I think I'm paralyzed.* Panic, anxiety, and helplessness pulse in a succession through wires in his head.

He works to calm himself. But there is an uneasiness. It is deep and bloating. He attempts to expel it by will. But can't. He sees the crash. It bursts wide, filling his brain. The noise is like swelling dowels pushing into his ears. He crashes again, and again, and again.

It stops. There's an opening in the yellow, and there's an irregular image of his wife Ellie's face. Although it is far away, it brings him warmth.

He remembers. Her doctor had called and said he needed to rush to the hospital as soon as he could. He'd asked for details, and the doctor said she had taken a turn for the worse and was failing. He'd been hurrying to see her at Lakeside Hospital, and now it appears he too is in a hospital, maybe even Lakeside. *How is she doing? Is she still alive?*

A familiar voice, someone he loves, grabs his attention. Despite his best focus, he only makes out an occasional word from his oldest son, Steve. "Accident . . . brain . . . prognosis . . . mother." He again strains to speak but can't.

Ellie is closer. His thoughts resonate within him. *Honey, I don't know what's wrong with me. But I need to see you one more time, before your disease takes you or my injuries take me. Hang on, darling, for me.*

Something has changed. The beeping has stopped. The yellow glow gone. He wonders what's happened. All is dead, silent, and colorless.

He senses he is no longer touching the bed. His body is strangely heavy and weightless at the same time. A distant radiance rushes toward him and flashes bright when it touches him. Then gone. Sight awakens, in all directions at once. Now suspended. Above him are fluorescent lights, and below, himself laying in a hospital bed; tubes and wires connected to medical devices. But the devices are quiet, as is his body. Both his sons are in the room. Robert is sitting, head down, hands clasped in his lap. Steve is standing next to him, with a hand on Robert's shoulder. A man and a woman in white jackets enter the room. Probably doctors. The woman is writing on a clipboard.

I'm having a near death experience. Exhilaration and fear vie for prominence.

I have to get back on my feet, and fast. I have to be with Ellie. I sense she's here, but waiting for me. She may not know why I'm not with her. That hurts.

Collection 16

He again looks upon his sons, and Ellie enters the room. He is surprised and relieved that she has recovered. While driving to the hospital, he'd wondered how he could ever live without her. He dreaded having to.

He'd always been attracted to her, from the first time he'd seen her at a friend's party twenty-five years ago. Over the years, they joked about how many people referred to their spouses or partners as soulmates. Yet, he and Ellie were certain they really were. That overwhelming, lifelong attraction he'd felt for her seems minimal compared to his feelings for her right now. As she gets nearer, she smiles, and it sends him strength. *She is angelic.*

Ellie touches the head of each of their sons, but they don't notice. She glides upward, and as she draws close to him says, "I love you," without speaking. The thought saturates every part of him. They'd married in their early twenties, and he thought he now knew everything about her. That no longer seems true. There are feelings being exchanged between them he'd never experienced with anyone before, not even her. They'd shared love, friendship, companionship, child rearing, and grief, but this goes beyond that, far beyond that. It is pure connection, in the strongest sense—a core coalescence.

He stares at his sons and is overwhelmed by the connection with them as well.

Somehow, the love among them all further intensifies, and he is the happiest he's ever been. He is at complete peace. No, he is peace.

Darkness.

In Sidney, Australia, a proud mother gives birth to fraternal twins: a boy, and a girl. They are destined to be close siblings.

Love is Everything

by **Joanna Michaels**

When I was a kid I attended Catholic school, and on Sundays I served as an altar boy at Saint James Church. I was a pretty good kid. Sure, I sometimes poked fun at kids who were fat, or who wore glasses, or had red hair, but my bullying never amounted to much more than a shove here or there. I grew up in the '50s. Things were different back then. Since the internet hadn't been invented, kids couldn't use Facebook to bully and torment others like some do today.

The last time I was inside of a church was on my wedding day—my first wedding day. An Elvis impersonator officiated my second marriage in Vegas. After that, I never set foot in church again. I never prayed again, either. I even forgot the words of all the prayers I had to memorize in school.

By the time I was forty, I had gone through one divorce and had been married twice. I had two kids—a boy and a girl. But to be honest, I wasn't a dutiful husband or father.

I probably committed every one of the seven deadly sins except for sloth. My wife calls me a germaphobe because everything around me needs to be spotless. So, tell me how the hell did I catch COVID?

When the pandemic hit, lots of people died. I mean, lots. And I think I was one of them. I say *I think* because all I know is one minute I'm lying in bed sick as a dog, struggling to breathe, and the next minute I'm floating on the ceiling of an ambulance looking down at my body. *Son of a bitch*, I thought, *I'm dead.*

I looked around for the tunnel that's supposed to whisk souls up to heaven, but there was just an open door that looked out into a hallway.

Collection 16

There was no light in the hall, but I stepped through the door to have a look around and BAM! The door slammed shut, scaring the crap outta me.

I continued walking down the hallway until I came to another open door. This one led to the outside. I stepped through, but it was foggy, dark, and I couldn't see much. Dilapidated buildings with broken windows surrounded the area. Some buildings stood partially demolished, and the trees along the street appeared black as if they had been burned. There was a scorched odor in the hazy air. The trees were leafless, and no grass was evident—just cracked concrete sidewalks with broken glass strewn about.

As I looked around, there was movement in the shadows. They began rising and moving toward me, and as they came closer, I spotted dirty, tattered clothes hanging from thin bodies. These people, or whatever they were, moved closer to me, their faces angry, and they held big sticks in their hands. I tried backing away, but they quickly surrounded me, pushing me from one person to another until they knocked me to the ground. Then they began beating me and kicking me. I held my arms over my head and cried out, "Somebody, help me, please!"

The crowd backed away, but one man moved forward. He looked more like a demon than a man. He reached his hand to me and pulled me upright. "What the hell!" I shouted.

"Exactly!" he said, his voice sounding like a growl. And then he laughed. Not a jovial laugh—a sinister laugh.

I looked up at him. He was at least a foot taller than me. "Oh, God!" I yelled, terrified by what stood before me.

The demon bellowed, "Never say that word down here! Never!"

"Down here?" I looked again at my surroundings—the broken streetlamps, overfilled garbage cans, burnt trees. "Am . . . am I, in h-hell?"

"Where else would you be?"

My eyes bugged out of my head. "You're the devil?"

He bowed. "You may call me Lucifer."

"No, no, no. This can't be. I was good . . . I think . . . Pretty good . . . Not bad enough to be sent to hell."

"Wrong!" He waved his arm, and a hologram appeared. It was a vision of the sacristy behind the main altar in the church where I served as altar boy. The hologram showed Father Francis as he turned away from me to put his vestment on. That's when I sneaked some of the Communion wine.

"That's my boy," said Lucifer.

Before I had a chance to deny it was me, another hologram materialized, and in this scene I'm sitting on a barstool in a saloon. I'm in my late twenties and married to my first wife. But she isn't with me. I gaze in horror as my drunk self attempts to seduce a young woman seated on the adjacent barstool. Her words and body language said to leave her alone, but I wouldn't stop. I got pretty handsy with her.

The devil grinned. "You were such a bad boy. Almost makes me weep with joy."

I covered my face with my hands and shouted, "No! Don't show me anymore."

"Oh, we're just getting started, boy." He rubbed his hands together, his fingers long and pointed.

The hologram changed once again, and I observed myself pocket cash from my friend's business after he asked me to watch over the cash register.

"You were a sneaky little fella," he bellowed.

"Stop!" I felt so ashamed. "I don't want to stay here." Turning away from him, I raised my hands to the dark sky and cried, "Jesus, please save me!"

In an instant, the brightest light I had ever seen appeared in front of me, and a figure stood in the center beckoning to me. I wasted no time jumping into the light. I fell to my knees at the feet of this man. Was it God, Jesus, an angel? I didn't know, but I clung to his robes and thanked him repeatedly for saving me from hell.

The dark fog had lifted, replaced by a beautiful meadow with flowers in colors I'd never seen before. Trees were lush with brilliant green leaves, and to my right a brook bubbled across stones while butterflies flitted among the flowers. The air tasted clean and sweet, and off in the distance I swore I could hear angels singing.

I stood and dusted off the dirt from the dark place I was in before and smiled. "This is more like it," I said. "This is heaven."

"My son," the figure said in a gentle voice. "I'm sorry. I can't let you stay here."

"Please don't send me back to hell. I'm sorry for all the bad things I did when I was alive. I should never have stopped going to church or believing in prayer. If you let me stay, I'll own up to every one of my sins and beg for forgiveness. Name my penance. I'll do anything you ask. Anything!"

He shook his head. "You did not need to go to church to find me, son. I've always been with you, and I know everything you've done, both good and bad. As a human, I gave you free will, and because you were a brave soul I sent you to live on Earth, the planet with the darkest energy. You had a purpose there, but you have not fulfilled it. Now you must go back and use the time you have left to be a better man. Learn to love, my son. Because love is everything."

I softly mumbled, "Love is everything."

"Oh, you're awake. How are you feeling?"

I opened my eyes. I was lying in a bed, a nurse at my side. "Where am I?" I croaked.

"You're in Saint James Hospital. You had COVID. Don't you remember?"

"I'm alive?"

She nodded. "You're very much alive."

"It hurts to swallow," I said, touching my throat.

"That's from the breathing tube."

"Wow, I had the craziest dream. I died and went to hell and then I was in Heaven, and all of a sudden, I'm here. On Earth. This is Earth, right?"

The nurse's expression was one of amusement. "Yes, this is Earth. How about I get the doctor for you?"

Tears stung my eyes. "Yeah, sure, get the doctor. In the meantime, where's my cell phone? I need to call my family—tell my wife and kids how much I love them."

Vanishing Color

by Micki Berthelot Morency

I roll off the mat and stretch the kinks out of my body. The sporadic snoring of my two younger brothers breaks the silence of the new day in the three-room house Papa built one room at a time like links on a bicycle chain. In the back, my parents sleep on the only bed in the house; my six-month old sister cocooned between them.

In the summer, I do my chores early in the morning. The July sun in the Haitian sky punishes everything that dares to step under it. Besides, it leaves me more time to spend with Abe before I will leave him behind soon to start middle school in the neighboring town. Our lone one-room school in the village fills heads less than halfway. The two teachers have limitations, just as the room bursts at the seams with too many students. Too often, I hear villagers tell each other that children are the savings accounts of the poor. Yet no one is getting rich, and this village should be a millionaire haven by now.

I shake my head and step into a pair of khaki shorts and a T-shirt emblazoned with the logo *Santé Sé Richess* from the American mission that brings medical care to the villagers twice a year. Except the mission hasn't brought neither health nor wealth to the community.

Barefoot, I open the door and raise my face to the fading dawn. I watch the moon fight its disappearance from the dark-gray sky. I tilt the plastic drum and dip an aluminum cup inside, scooping enough water to brush my teeth and wash my face before grabbing the bucket and making my way across the road.

Abe's green suit blends into the leaves of the bean trees, but the white ball in his hands pierces the darkness. His face barely visible, he smiles when I kick the front tire of his rusty bike.

"Hey." I fist-bump him through his lizard's paw. "Gotta fetch water," I say. "Mama's washing bed sheets and towels today."

"Oh, I can make it to the river," Abe says, bouncing the ball between his covered hands. "We can play on the lot behind the church."

Collection 16

I poke the rear tire now and frown. "I'm not carrying you like the last time if that thing exhales its last breath."

We laugh. But I hear pain on the tail end of his fading voice. "It'll make it," he says. "Come on. Let's go."

"Abe, why don't we play with the team later? You can't hide inside that costume forever."

"And why not?" He sniffs. "No one wants to play with me, except you."

"I'll make them. You know I can."

He hoists himself over the bike and pedals, and I skip next to him like I'd been doing since we were in kindergarten except then we used to race each other to school.

A few years ago, Abe's skin started to change color and break like leather left in the sun too long. In the beginning, we laughed about it, and he called himself "polka-dot." Then he stopped wearing his school uniform because the navy-blue shorts and the short-sleeve shirt didn't cover his changing skin. The sun was merciless on the white spots all over his body as if it were trying to chase them away. Kids teased him. I beat them up.

Within a couple weeks, he lost all his blackness until he looked like the white missionaries who come from Florida to our local clinic to treat worms, skin rash, diarrhea, and everything with no name. But they could not bring Abe's black skin back, so they brought him special suits and sunscreen that allowed him to venture outside.

Last year, he saw a picture of a green lizard in one of the books the missionaries brought to the small library in the back of the clinic. The books were written in English, but the pictures of action figures, fancy cars, and rare animals fascinated the boys. Abe asked them for a lizard suit. And when his feet were too sore to walk, they brought him a bike.

I think the suit is cool.

"I'm gonna miss you . . . um . . . and Martine," Abe says, clearing his throat as he turns to look at me. "She likes you, Eddy."

"No. Not me." I wink at him.

He's so white now that I expect him to speak Créole with an accent like the missionaries. "I'll miss you, too," I say, resting my hand on his knee. He stops pedaling.

Metamorphosis

"You know, Eddy, I used to hate being so dark. Remember the kids called me "Midnight." I wanted to be brown like you . . ."

"But we're all Black, no matter the shade," I say, patting his knee lightly. It's as if someone had turned Abe's skin inside out.

"If we're all Black, then why do we look so different from each other. Martine is almost yellow like a ripe summer mango."

I smile. "Well, Abe, this is a question for the pastor. I suppose he can ask God." I shrug, but I'm thinking about a ripe mango and lick my lips, tasting salt from the sweat coursing around my mouth. "I don't have an answer for that."

I reach for a low-hanging soursop from a tree on the side of the road. I bite into it and hand it to Abe who passes it over after ripping a juicy chunk off the fruit. We eat it in a silence broken by the spitting sound of the skin and the black seeds.

Back on the road, dry twigs snap under the tires of the bike. "I can carry you to school, Abe. It's not that far." I flex my biceps. "I don't like the idea of starting middle school without you. You're my best friend, Lizard Man."

He stops the bike in the back of the church and pushes the hood of the suit away from his face. Stray black dots cling to his skin in a stubborn fight to resist their departure. "I'd rather die, Eddy, than mount you every day like a donkey to go to school."

He spits on the ground. "You'll be my teacher in the evening, right?" He stares at me. "Um . . . Martine promises to come by and help me too."

"I knew it." I punch his upper arm lightly. "Martine likes *you*." I point my index finger at his narrowed eyes.

"No. She likes the new me." The grimace creases Abe's face like an accordion. "She said I look almost white now. I don't like what I've become. I'll never be me again, Eddy." He kicks the sand and winces. "I want to get out of this stupid suit. I want to go to school like everyone else. I want my midnight skin back," he yells.

"But . . . you . . ." I close my mouth, not knowing what to say. People do look at Abe as if his essence has disappeared along with his skin color. Papa said changes are inevitable in life, but not when life turns you into a stranger you don't like. Then who are you?

Abe throws the ball hard at me. I hit it back. The bicycle standing between us as a net.

The game begins. He disappears into the lizard suit.

Metamorphosis

by Mark H. Newhouse

"I'm telling you the truth," I shouted to the detective. "Warn everyone." Lieutenant Stern uncrossed her legs.

I was no longer interested in a tall blonde's physical attributes. I leaned forward, eager to hear what she was going to do. "Officer, didn't you hear me?"

Stern tapped her long, red, polished nails on the tablet keyboard.

Panic set in, a vise tightening on my heart. "You must do something. It could happen to you. Stop with that tablet!"

My wife, Lisa, was sitting opposite the detective. "No. I do not know what happened to John." She said and pulled the robe tighter over her negligee.

"How much was this waste of my money?" I demanded. Why was she ignoring me? "How much?" I yelled louder.

"We had . . . have . . . a solid marriage," Lisa said and added, "For the most part."

How can she tell a stranger that?

"Was he having an affair?" Stern stopped typing.

What nerve! I should have left the room right after the detective asked that, but I was immobile. "Go ahead, tell her the truth," I said.

"I . . . don't know."

The detective clicked her nails on the tablet's screen. "Everything you say is confidential," she said.

"Don't say another word," I shouted.

Lisa sighed. "I don't know. He was on his phone all the time—"

"Yes. I was," I interrupted. "I was on my damn phone! It was business."

The detective shook her head and typed, *possible affair*, on her tablet. "Do you suspect anyone?" She stopped typing. "Speak your mind."

"You imbecilic idiot!" I wanted to choke her with her string of fake pearls. "There was no other woman!"

Linda's face turned hard. "Shirley Watson, his secretary. He was always on the phone with her."

"What? Wacky Watson? Are you joking?" Again, if I could have, I would have stormed out. I was stuck on the couch, forced to listen to this gibberish.

Click, click, click . . .

The clicking of Stern's nails on the keyboard was annoying. I wanted to chop off Stern's fingers. "Listen, you are wasting time," I said, trying to sound more patient than I felt. "Lisa, you know I am not the type to risk financial ruin with some sordid affair—"

"What about enemies?" The detective picked up a framed photograph of Lisa and me at our wedding twenty years ago. "Successful men make enemies—"

Lisa shook her head. "Not him. He was cautious . . . never did anything that would upset anyone."

"You got something right." I fumed, wishing they would let me speak. "You have this all wrong," I said. "There wasn't any affair. No enemies."

Lisa chuckled. "John never did anything wrong. He was . . . kind of boring. You know what I mean."

"Me boring? You are the one who's boring," I shouted. Of all the things I had to listen to, "boring" cut me the most. "You're laughing? At me?" These two females were denigrating this investigation as if it were the start of a beautiful friendship between them. What would my traitorous wife reveal about me next?

Detective Stern purred, "Boring? As in the boudoir?"

Was that in her list of rehearsed questions? Did I detect a spark of humanity? Vulgar curiosity? Had she leaned forward, blue eyes wider and ears perked up like some dog waiting for a morsel worthy of sharing about my sex life? "Tell her the truth! I am . . . was a tiger in bed."

Lisa sighed and then nodded.

"I see," Stern said and returned to her blasted typing.

My mouth dropped open. They had it all wrong.

"You have a lovely home," Stern said.

Collection 16

"John was an adequate provider." Lisa flashed her two-carat diamond ring at Stern. "I can't complain about that."

"Good investment, a house, a diamond," I said. "For you! I get nothing if I can't get out of this—"

"And you said nothing is missing."

"No. Just John."

I glowered at her dramatically long sigh. "Just John?"

"What about his car?"

"My Jag? It had better not be missing!" I wanted to run to the garage and check my vintage XKE had not been taken. Lisa's hand landed on top of me. It stopped me cold.

"He loved that car . . . more than me. He'll kill me if something happens to it."

"So, his car is here. And your car?"

"It is here too. I don't understand how he could simply vanish like this."

"Did he ever do it before?"

"Never. Sometimes, I wished—"

"What did you wish?" I wanted to explode, but all my emotions were locked inside. These two were talking about me as if I were not in the room. I could hear every word. I saw every movement through the glass screen: my eye to this blurry world.

"Children?"

Lisa cleared her throat. "John didn't want any."

"*We* didn't want them! You and I decided," I shouted.

"Did you want children?"

"Sure. When we were younger . . . we had nothing then." Lisa looked at a photograph of me receiving a medal from the mayor. "He was successful . . . in business."

"Damn right!" I was glad she finally showed some recognition of my accomplishments.

Stern closed the cover of her tablet. "I have enough for now. There weren't any signs of forced entry."

"John had a burglar alarm installed. He said it was the best." Lisa led Stern to the control panel. "I checked the video. One second, he was on his cell phone; the next, he was gone."

Lisa's right. I was on my phone. Totally, unsuspecting.

"Forensics found no blood. No sign of a struggle," Stern said.

Metamorphosis

I struggled. It was no use. It was as if powerful magnets were pulling me. I couldn't break away. My whole body was changing. I tried to hold on.

"Well, this is quite a mystery," Stern said. "I'll take his phone with me—"

"John won't like that. He never lets me touch it—"

Stern reached down. "Ma'am, Lisa, we need to check every call. Your husband vanished without a clue—"

"Yes. Check this phone," I shouted. "At last, you're on the right track." I felt hopeful as Stern lifted my phone from the couch. She was in for a big surprise. Huge! I would make her hear me. I would find a way to tell her the damn thing trapped me. I would warn the world that these electronic monsters were just waiting for the right time to suck us into their guts and change us—"

"Bag this phone," Stern ordered a uniformed cop.

I saw the plastic bag whip out from his pocket. "No! No! No!" I felt plastic gloves pick me up with two fingers. I saw the open transparent bag as I was carried toward its maw.

"John won't like you taking his phone," Lisa said.

"Thank you, dear wife." I was relieved. She saved me from the baggie and the male cop's clumsy fingers. God knows what would happen to me if he dropped the phone on our sparkling porcelain tiled floor where I'd witnessed countless dishes explode into millions of bits of glass.

"Lisa, you need to understand this is a missing person investigation," Stern said. "We need to examine every possibility. Bag the phone, now."

The clear plastic opening of the bag was like the wide-open mouth of a shark. No teeth, but deadly. "No!" The stupid, deaf cop dropped me into the bag. I stared desperately through the polyethylene. "I'm in here. Please?"

The cop pinched the bag shut.

Stern stuck a handwritten evidence label on the flap.

I was trapped. The oxygen will run out. I'll fight for air . . . suffocate. "HELP ME!" I typed on the keyboard. I was gulping. Air. Barely human, I kicked the side of the case. They had to hear me!

"It's vibrating," Lisa said.

"She heard it. I'm saved."

"Wait. It stopped." Lisa's eyes were huge staring into the bag.

"It's dead," Stern replied.

For once, she was right.

Rotag

by **David M. Pearce**

My pulse raced. I pushed my way to get to my place among the throng. A bandmate jogged through a gantlet of bright white, orange, and blue uniforms; her white glove high-fiving through the packed space, the other hand clutching her silver trombone. She laughed and hollered, weaving between columns and rows. Her eyes sparkled, teeth flashed, and she bounced on her toes.

She winked and slapped my outstretched hand. "Go Gators!"

"Go Gators!" I replied. It seemed the appropriate thing to say.

We'd gathered underneath the corner of the stadium. Overhead, gray concrete slabs, their construction akin to an upside-down step pyramid, shielded us from the sun. From the grassy field beyond, a mélange of scents—mowed grass mingled with the lingering chemical stink of fertilizer—wafted through the tunnel.

My throat itched. I had been sick with a summer cold most of the week, and the heat wasn't doing me any favors. If I could find my spot, I'd avoid freaking out. Wasn't I supposed to be closer to the front?

I ducked around another joyous bandmate, frantically searching.

"Let's go, let's go!" The drum major herded us against the tunnel wall. He glared, trying to prompt movement. "Get with your squads!"

It was pregame, minutes before kickoff, the first contest of the season. The band uniform weighed a ton: a polyester cocoon. Sweat dampened the back of my neck. I coughed into my hand, trying to find air. Where the hell were my peeps?

My mind flashed back to the band tryout several weeks ago, a nervous encounter with the band director. Somehow, I muddled through. Upperclassmen dubbed all freshmen in the Pride of the Sunshine with the moniker Rotag. It's a harmless label . . . mostly harmless. But you're not a Gator yet. Not until you've gone through tryouts, band camp, and the weeks of practice before the first game.

And so, I spent countless hours learning new drills, which included the pregame ritual and a halftime show. March forward sixteen steps. Float eight. Pause sixteen beats. Float another eight. On and on.

We fought heatstroke, dodged summer thunderstorms, swatted away mosquitoes and fire ants, all while our legs turned to jelly—marching—up the field, back, into familiar formations. One, two, red-eye, go.

With the cold medicine I'd taken earlier, my head swam. But there was no way I'd miss this day. Not after working so hard to get here. If only I could remember where I'm supposed to be—

A vise grip landed on my elbow and spun me around. My squad leader, Rob, smirked. He stared at me over his sunglasses, then pointed to the spot beside him with his trumpet. "Right here, Rotag." But his voice lacked the heat the slur carried many weeks ago. He dragged me into place beside him.

I heaved a sigh.

My other squad mates chuckled. A girl with black curly hair nodded—Melissa, another freshman. How could she be so calm?

Melissa frowned. "You okay, Brian? You look pale."

I gave her my best smile. No need for my squad mates to know I felt miserable. We're supposed to be a team. If I told them I was sick, they'd never let me take the field. And that would leave a hole in the formation. No way I would let that happen. "Just nervous." I wiped the sweat off my face. "Can it get any hotter?"

"Just remember not to lock your knees on the field," Rob said.

I nodded. It's one of the first things they tell you in band camp. The minute you unlock your knees after standing around in the heat, the flush of blood to your head could cause you to pass out. It would be worse with my impaired constitution; I feared dropping midfield during the performance. "I'll remember."

The roar of the crowd came and went, the reason unknown to us here inside the tunnel.

"Glad you found us, man." Chris had been in the band longer than I can imagine—a graduate student with a scraggly red beard. "I would hate to leave you behind."

Collection 16

"Cripes." I swallowed hard. "How do you find anything in this mess?"

"You get used to it." Rob rubbed a water spot off the plating of his horn where a drop of sweat had landed. He and Chris had done this before, many times. He craned his neck, standing on his toes, gazing toward the tunnel exit. "Any minute now."

I really could have used a tissue to unclog my airways. "Guess it's the wrong time to ask if I can use the restroom?"

My squad leader rolled his eyes.

Chris reached up and adjusted the plume on Rob's hat. The aptly named "dead chicken" wanted to keel over.

"Thanks, kemosabe."

"De nada."

Melissa fanned her face with one hand. "I don't know why you keep calling him that. Doesn't kemosabe mean *idiot* in Apache?"

Rob smirked. "And? My fraternity brother is an idiot."

"Takes one to know one." Chris shrugged.

Rob gave him the finger. "Screw you."

"What's taking so long?" Their banter had me on edge.

Chris shrugged again. "Television coverage. Everything needs to happen at just the right time and then we'll take the field."

"Will they show the band on TV?" Melissa asked.

"Maybe a small part of the pregame," Chris replied.

My collar tightened around my throat. I coughed. "Is it always like this?"

Melissa frowned. "Like what?"

"I feel lightheaded." In truth, I worried I might collapse at any moment.

Rob nodded. "Yeah."

"Are you sure you're okay?" Melissa asked. "You don't look well."

I deliberately ignored her question. Not now. Not when I was so close to getting through the turmoil. "Why do we—"

"Band! Ten-hut!" We couldn't see the drum major from there, so the call went out down the line. *Boom-boom.* The entire drumline reacted; their raps pealed like thunder.

We snapped to attention. Gazes fixed; we stared straight ahead. Elbows pointed. Horns held in perfect alignment.

"Here we go! Here we go!" A second drum major raced to the head of the columns. Excitement raged through the band, a living thing demanding to be set loose.

A fat drop of sweat rolled to the tip of my nose and stayed there. I wanted so badly to wipe it away, but I dared not. Not while I was at attention. I breathed through my mouth, trying to get oxygen.

Twee-eet. Tweet. Tweet. Tweet. Tweet. RAT-tat-tat-tat. The drum major's whistle and lead snare announced the roll off. My heart leapt into my throat. A cadence began, and the other drums drowned out all other sounds. My feet moved in time with the beat. A crowd of tens of thousands roared from inside the stadium.

The column surged. Our feet flew, toes pointed in a chop step. I moved with the others, concentrating on staying in line, watching Rob out of the corner of my eye to make sure I didn't get too far ahead or behind him.

The tunnel gave way to blinding light. Thank goodness I memorized the music; there's no way I could read it through the perspiration pouring through my vision.

The afternoon sun was merciless, but it didn't matter. We raced into the end zone, rows and columns forming up, extending sideline to sideline. I found my spot, legs pumping as I marked time. There were people in the crowd, but, to me, they were a blur.

The stadium announcement blared through the overhead speakers. "Ladies and gentlemen, the Pride of the Sunshine State, the University of Florida Fightin' Gator Marching Band!"

Rat-tat. Rat-tat. Rat-tat-tatta-tatta-tat-tat.

Horns. Are. Up. An explosion of sound erupted. On wobbly legs, I poured all my energy into the song. Joy flooded through me: a primal ecstasy. The opening fanfare of the *Jaws* theme was an angelic chorus. The crowd joined us in a cheer. There's a second roll off and then we marched eight-to-five, playing "Orange and Blue." My heart soared.

I was one of many, no longer a Rotag.

Something from a Small Moon

by William R. Platt

I work the late shift at a dingy little place called the Rock Hopper Saloon down at the back end of the asteroid. Most nights are pretty quiet. The scavengers and smugglers who hang out there don't have much to celebrate.

My shift had just begun when I noticed the scavenger staring into his beer. Willy and his partner, Mezzo, are famous for ringing up big bar tabs and then disappearing without paying. I worked my way over, wiping down the bar with a towel.

"Hiya, Willy. Where's Mezzo?"

I scared him. His head bobbed up out of a stupor and he pulled his arm close. Something gurgled deep in his chest. Bloodshot eyes gaped at me.

"Mezzo ain't here, Ray." He spat the words out and lowered his gaze back into his glass.

This wasn't the same man I'd seen a hundred times before. Something was gnawing at him.

"No offense, Willy, but can you pay for that beer?"

He stretched his hand over the scanner and let the bar count his credits, pulling it away when the total reached six mil.

"Holy shit, Willy, you could buy your own asteroid. Did you find something special?"

Willy swirled the beer around the bottom of his glass and drained it in a gulp. His eyes bounced around the room.

"Boridium, lots of it. Took all I could carry."

Boridium is the most precious element in the solar system. Physicists have found a way to infuse the stuff with tachyons enabling spacecraft to

Metamorphosis

reach incredible speeds. Faster-than-light travel is right around the corner, if we can find enough boridium.

I leaned in. "Boridium! Is it still there? C'mon, let's go get it."

Willy jerked upright. "No way, I can't go back there." His head twitched like a jittery rooster.

I poured him another beer and pushed it across the bar. "Why? What the hell happened?"

He took a deep breath and exhaled slowly. It smelled like graphite, oil, and beer.

"Mezzo and me found a shipwreck on a moon the other side of Jupiter. The readings on the scanner showed a huge cache of boridium, the purest I've ever seen. Mezzo was scared, but I figured this was our shot at a real payday, so I took us in."

"What scared Mezzo?"

"That ship wasn't made by humans."

"What? You think it's aliens?"

"It's gotta be. It's a big, black ball made from a metal that don't reflect any light. There's no markings on its hull, no letters or numbers. Just streaks of frozen water vapor and methane. It was cold and dark and dead, like it crashed there a billion years ago."

"It was hauling boridium?"

"No, more like it ran on the stuff. We got in through a hole in the hull and found the boridium stacked near something that looked like a fusion reactor. The inside of that ship is crazier than the outside. There's no crew quarters, no bridge, not even a friggin' chair, nothing but wires, pipes, and circuitry. We had to cut our way through with acetylene torches."

Something inside him caused Willy to start coughing. He hacked a wad of dark mucus into his palm and wiped it on his pants. Pills skittered across the bar when he popped the lid on a small plastic bottle. He washed down a handful with a gulp of beer.

"How'd you get the boridium out?"

"Mezzo carried it to the opening while I stayed outside and loaded our ship. When we were full, I called him to come out. He didn't answer, so I went back in looking for him. Things had changed. The frost had melted, and steam was coming off the conduits. Lights were blinking on and off. That ship was coming alive."

Collection 16

Willy drained his beer and slid his glass to me for a refill. His arm shook so badly he had to hold it in place with his other hand. I poured him another beer.

"What happened then?"

"I found Mezzo about halfway to the reactor trussed up on crossbars shaped like an *X*." Willy wiped a black ball of snot from his nose. "A mess of wiry tentacles tied down his arms and legs. His helmet was gone and his suit was ripped to shreds. Hoses full of red, brown, and yellow fluids ran out of his body. That ship was feeding on him, pumping all the liquids out of his body."

His arm shot out and knocked the glass of beer from the bar, shattering it on the floor.

"Damn, Willy, take it easy."

"Mezzo was still alive, Ray. I don't know how 'cause there weren't no air. He looked straight at me and tried to talk. I couldn't hear nothin', but he was asking me for help."

"You're gonna be all right."

"No, I ain't, Ray. One of them tentacles shot out of the wall and wrapped around my arm like a python. It must've been full of needles or something because it bit me right through my pressure suit."

Willy lifted his left sleeve. Ugly yellow blisters and red puncture wounds spiraled from elbow to wrist. Something throbbed beneath his skin.

"What the hell . . .?"

"I blasted the damn thing with my torch, but more tentacles came after me. I burned some of them with the torch, but there were too many. I left Mezzo behind and ran like hell."

His breathing came in short, rapid gasps. He began to shudder.

"More of them tentacles were busy on the outside, adjusting antennae and signal dishes. It's probably a probe or a beacon. I don't know. I got the hell out."

"Take it easy, Willy."

"I left Mezzo behind, Ray. What kind of friend does that?" Willy buried his head in his sleeve and sobbed.

"It's okay, Willy. You did what anyone would do. How long ago was that?"

He raised his head and wiped black oily tears across his face.

"Three days, maybe four. I ain't slept much. My arm hurts and these painkillers don't work."

"You told anyone else?"

"No way, I can't go back there."

"It's important, Willy. You gotta tell someone."

A miner watching a ballgame called to me from the other end of the bar. "Yo, Ray, turn it up. Something's happened."

A concerned woman, one of those Breaking-News personalities, filled the screens. I found the remote and turned up the volume.

". . . entering our solar system. Their origin is unknown, but the authorities are certain these objects are not of human design. They are decelerating from faster-than-light speeds on trajectories that will bring them into the inner solar system. A swarm of alien objects numbering hundreds of millions, perhaps billions, is heading directly for us . . ."

"HahahahAaaaaaahHahahahaah!"

Willy screamed and laughed at the same time. He stumbled away from the bar. His arm flailed above his head, spinning him around.

"My arm, Ray, I can't control it!"

His outstretched limb rushed toward me, dragging Willy like a puppet. I fell to the floor as he slammed against the bar. His arm pulled him over the top. The whites of his eyes were completely black.

"Do something, Ray!"

I reached up.

Tentacles burst through his skin and wrapped around my forearm. Thousands of tiny needles pierced my skin. I grabbed a vodka bottle and pounded. It released me in a shower of glass and liquor.

I scuttled to the front of the bar, cradling my arm against my chest. Dark-silver rivulets seeped from the injection wounds. I wiped the fluid away and tripped over a chair. A man running for the doorway jumped past me. Something in my body wanted to reach out and grab him. That something wasn't me.

Thick mechanical tentacles coiled around Willy's chest, pinning him against the wall. Dozens of tendrils from his arms and legs slithered into the ventilation and cyber optics.

"Ray!"

Black greasy fluids dripped from his eyes and mouth as the coils tightened around his body. I couldn't tell if he was crying or laughing. His voice sounded like something from another world.

"It's too late, Ray. We're coming. Everything is gonna change."

I left Willy behind and ran like hell.

Masterpiece
by K. L. Small

With her pulse thumping, Delaney hesitated before gingerly pressing her age-spotted hand against the art studio's busted door. It swung open, groaning on broken hinges. She gasped.

Paper littered the floor. The drawers of her art supply cabinet lay empty in a chaotic pile beside her overturned drafting table. A puddle spread from toppled water containers.

Her eyes darted to the display wall where her finished painting should be. Gone.

Her hand flew to her mouth.

Footsteps echoed in the hallway behind her. She spun around, afraid the thief had returned. In relief, she recognized her business manager sauntering toward her.

"Good morning, Delaney." A broad smile lit his face. "I'm here to pick up your portrait for the Legacy Exhibition."

"Andrew." Her voice quivered. "The studio was robbed. The painting's gone."

He peered into the studio and frowned. "Have you called the police?"

Delaney shook her head. "I just got here."

She stepped past the damaged door, shuddering at the violation of her creative space. Despite her arthritis, she bent down and righted the water containers.

She blinked back tears. "Why would someone do this?"

"Money. You're a successful artist. The stolen pieces will wind up on the black market. What did they get?"

"At least a dozen unframed paintings." Delaney gestured at the shelf barren of her artwork. She exhaled slowly. "And the self-portrait for the exhibition."

"Thank goodness most of your collection is already there."

Delaney balled her hands into fists. "I worked so hard on that self-portrait."

"Do you have another one? Something at home?"

She glared at him. "I hate self-portraits. I only did it because the Legacy demanded one."

Andrew stroked his chin. "You used to do them, years ago, before you took up your dark architectural style."

"No one wants a watercolor of an old hag." She stooped stiffly to pick up sheets of paper from the floor.

"Delaney," Andrew scolded, "I wish you saw the beautiful, creative person the rest of the world sees."

With a snicker, she brushed a strand of white hair away from her eyes. "Maybe long ago."

Andrew shrugged. "But right now, I need a painting of you."

"It's too late to start over," Delaney said. "Much too late."

"The exhibition contract requires a self-portrait. There's a steep penalty for failure to perform." His eyes were apologetic. "You better start painting."

Delaney clenched her teeth and balled her hands into fists. "My paints and brushes are gone."

"Get new ones. I'll be back tomorrow." Andrew carefully stepped over the spilled water and left.

After the police had come and gone, Delaney tried to restore order to the studio. While she cleaned, she worried about how to recreate a painting that had taken her two weeks to complete. It couldn't be done without paints and brushes. She had no choice, though. While a contractor replaced the door, Delaney went shopping.

Shay's House of Fine Art Supplies stood a few blocks from her studio. The owner's knowledge of quality paints, papers, and brushes was the reason she had rented in the area. The familiar set of bells over the door jangled gaily, announcing her arrival. The aroma of solvents and paints filled the space. Racks of canvasses and sketchpads lined one wall, and bins of paint brushes stood ahead of her.

"Shay, I need your help," she called anxiously and shuffled to the counter. The hurried pace to get to the shop had left her winded.

"He's not here," a young man at the cash register said. "He had a family emergency."

Delaney leaned against the countertop and caught her breath. "I'm sorry to hear that, but I need supplies."

"I'll be glad to find them for you."

"Shay usually has my supplies set aside."

"Good," he said. "What's the name and I'll check."

"Delaney."

His eyes widened. "You're the famous Delaney? Shay talks about you all the time." He smiled shyly. "I teased him that he must be in love with the beautiful Delaney."

With her cheeks warming, she shook her head. "His eyesight is worse than I thought. He must not be able to see all the white hair and wrinkles."

He laughed nervously. "Shay told me you get anything you need."

The young man rummaged through boxes and tins behind the counter. "I found it." He placed a cardboard box bearing her name and a leather case on the counter.

She opened the box to expose a dozen tubes of watercolor paint, more vibrant colors than she usually employed. She opened the leather case and stared at the paintbrush's silver bristles. As she stroked the bristles, her heart beat faster and a tingle ran through her fingertips.

"This isn't the brush I use."

"It was on top of the box." The young man shrugged. "You can leave it if you don't want it."

Delaney weighed her option. "I need a brush, and if Shay saved it for me, I'll take it."

Back at her studio, Delaney examined the handmade paintbrush. As she grasped the wooden handle, vibrations pulsed through her fingertips. The feeling frightened but intrigued her.

She squeezed the watercolor paints on her palette and added water, swirling the mixtures together with her new brush. Rich aromas rose from the paints. She inhaled and lowered her brush into the familiar gray puddle of paint she used in her somber urban scenes. The bristles filled with the dull color. She swiped the brush across the paper and delighted in the way it slid across the surface.

When she returned to the palette for more paint, a sensation shot up her arm, and the brush moved straight to the red paint. She fought the motion, but the brush pulled straight to the pool of paint. With a full brush, red ribbons of color splashed across her paper, accompanied by the swish of satin fabric. A long billowing dress appeared in the painting.

As night darkened the studio, Delaney turned on lights and examined her incomplete artwork. The vivid colors and freedom of the image—so unlike her usual style—made her smile. A surge of energy flooded through her. Her arthritis pain melted away. A stray piece of hair—no longer white, but auburn—fell across her face.

Next, the brush raced to the green paint, and she smelled evergreens. Trees spread across the painting's background in a splash of intense colors. For hours, the colors exploded across the watercolor paper. A passion for painting filled every cell of her body.

As sunrise brightened the studio, the brush dipped into flesh tones, and Delaney felt herself pulled into the paper. She closed her eyes and let the feeling carry her into the scene with the paintbrush in her hand. The red dress swirled around her legs, and the tree branches swept across her cheek.

In the afternoon, Andrew knocked on the new studio door.

"I'm here for the painting," he called. When there was no answer, he tried the knob, and the door swung open.

He stepped inside the workspace determined to collect Delaney's self-portrait for the exhibition. Surprised not to see the artist, his gaze fixed on the display wall. Stepping closer, he marveled at the painting of a youthful Delaney wearing a flaming-red dress, dancing in a forest. Locks of auburn hair floated around her glowing face. Her eyes glittered with laughter, and she smiled directly at him. An involuntary whistle escaped his lips.

"It's a masterpiece!"

In awe, he stepped back and bumped into a work table. He reached out to steady himself, and his hand brushed against a leather packet with an image of a paintbrush on one side. He stared at the label and read it aloud. "Made from unicorn hair."

Andrew opened the leather case, but it was empty. He glanced at the painting again and noticed a silver-haired paintbrush in Delaney's hand.

With his suspicion growing, he moved closer to the portrait. The red dress fluttered as if ruffled by a breeze. Delaney winked at him and raised a hand in farewell.

The Wave

by Minda A. Stephens

Phuket, Thailand, 2004

Sunshine washed golden on the shoreline the first afternoon I saw them together. She arrived first, then he joined her at the resort bar. They slipped away for a walk just before sunset. At a distance, the beach framed them while the surf slid in gentle layers around their feet. They walked in tandem like two egrets: graceful, ethereal, ready to take flight. And here I was, hired to watch them.

I shot pictures of their movements for the remainder of that day. All these years as a cameraman and I still find it remarkable how you can tell when two people are in love, even at the distance of a football field, no matter who the people are. I think there must be a glimpse of the eternal in it.

My employer hadn't exactly seen it that way. "I want the money shot! Do you understand me?" said Rick, private investigator to the morally insolvent. "If they weren't three thousand miles away, I'd do it myself." He slugged down yet another shot of whiskey, then belched.

This was supposed to be a slam-dunk luxury assignment. I would stay at a five-star hotel, get some tell-all photos of them together, and the money would be wired to my account back home. Under-the-table payment—maybe—but who would *that* hurt? Not my family. We had said our goodbyes on December 22. My kids were older and always spent Christmas with my ex. Besides, they were used to seeing the back of me. I'd been an on-call cameraman at WFAW for fifteen years before merciless budget cuts at the station and desperation made me a free agent.

Metamorphosis

For two days I followed them around like an unseen homeless dog. When he noticed me, he approached to see what I was doing. I told him I worked for *Call of Nature Magazine*. I even showed him some seascapes I'd taken that day. I got the impression that: a) he did not believe my cover story, and b) he would have paid far better than Rick's agency. But that would have made things way more complicated.

December 25 came, and I called my family safe in the knowledge I could make my mortgage payment. Then came the morning of the twenty-sixth. I started tracking them at 6:30 a.m. Now it was 7:50, and they were in my viewfinder crosshair.

I lifted my camera, like a voyeur who thinks he is part of something that has nothing whatsoever to do with him. But I was *not* a voyeur. My part of this affair was *purely* commercial. Perched from the balcony of their hotel, I held them in fast focus with my 200-600mm zoom lens. At one point she ran a few meters ahead. I clicked stills of her. Then she returned to him. Each held the other's gaze, and finally . . . they kissed. "Yes," I whispered, "That's it! Gotcha!"

The woman was the first to notice a change in the surf. He kept walking, then she said something to him. They stopped and stared at the water draining from the shore, then grasped hands and started running inland. This time, I set the camera on video. They ran faster and faster. Soon they were lost in the panicked crowd rushing inland. I lifted the lens up to see a long wave on the horizon. At a distance it appeared harmless. Then it began devouring everything in its path, churning boats and beach cabanas into its trough, slamming them down, then pulling them under its crest.

I stood up and set a wide focus on the camera. "Run! Run!" I shouted. But the wave enveloped everything. There was no time to stop. I followed it with my sight as it moved onshore consuming houses, cars, vendor stands, and yet more people.

Then came the whine of buildings around me. Glass and wood and steel were slowly buckling, breaking, and blending into the onslaught of watery rubbish that swallowed up beach blankets, elegant resort furniture, café tables and chairs, landscaping—everything. People were falling and going under, others trying to reach into the debris and save them. My hands shook as I viewed the scene. I fled down the external hallway of the building in search of refuge and finally happened upon a stairway that led to the rooftop. There, I strapped my second camera onto a column and sent the focus down to the debris and bodies floating three stories below. The cries for help. The cries for salvation. I hear their voices to this day.

Suddenly, I realized that I was not alone. A dozen ragged children surrounded me. There was a young woman with a terrified toddler looking at me in desperation. I turned and adjusted my camera to keep it recording as buildings collapsed into the melting-pot sludge of civilization beneath us.

Then it happened.

The noise of the melee below was drowned out by the all-to-familiar sound of a news chopper. I unstrapped the camera and raised it up to signal I was with the media. They sent down a rescue basket to pull me to safety.

I looked at the hapless children and considered my next move. Then I recruited an older child to hold the camera steady and keep filming. I loaded the woman with the baby and two small kids first and sent the others up in their turn—two to four at a time, depending on their size. The helicopter left and returned. On the return trip, I boarded the basket to safety.

Turns out it was a CCN Broadcasting helicopter. A producer was onboard. She asked if I was on assignment. "Not *anymore*," I answered. The network purchased my tsunami footage and hired me on the spot to film for the rest of the day and the days that followed.

As I worked, I stopped and talked to survivors. The morning after my rooftop rescue, I read the posted list of the missing and the dead. Her body had been found amid the rubble.

Rick finally reached me the following week. "They're settling up her estate," he said. "Did you get evidence of the affair? Tabloids are calling me nonstop! They'll buy anything ya got. You'll get a huge fee. Life-changing! My commission from the ex-husband alone is life-changing! Did you get the money shot?"

I was walking past the identification board that now posted pictures of missing victims. I saw his picture. People, still raw with grief and shock,

Metamorphosis

bumped past me. I felt warmth radiating from a fire burning in a barrel outside a nearby refuge shelter. While Rick ranted like a rooster discovering an empty henhouse, I took out my camera one, opened the files, and scrolled the images of them walking on the beach moments before the disaster. The files were labeled and organized, ready to be sent to the voice bristling obscenities onto the airwaves from the other side of the world. I paused to view the shot of them kissing. The tabloid money shot. The pay-for-the-kids-college and retire-mortgage-free shot.

"Rick, you're breaking up. Listen." I paused to think up a story. "When the tsunami hit, I had to scramble from my room, and camera one was missing from my bag. I went back to find it, and there were bodies and debris where my hotel had been."

"What! Do you expect payment for an assignment you didn't even complete? Wait. Wait! They're doing retrospectives of her work. Do you have any last shots of her alive? Or, better yet, dead?"

"I just told you that camera was lost along with all the material on it."

Rick kept bellowing while I studied a still of her from the last day of her life. She was radiant, ebullient as she twirled in the sand, water splashing under her feet. Glowing light reflected up onto her face. If I do say so myself, it was a *perfect* exposure. Perfect.

Unbeknownst to Rick, I had already sent that picture to her parents while posing as an anonymous fan who had seen every one of her movies.

"Hello. Hello!" he yelled. "Did you get *any* pictures?"

I closed the files, pressed delete, ejected the memory card, and threw it into the fire.

"No," I said, "I didn't get a thing." Then I hung up.

The Timekeeper's Garden

by Mike Summers

In the tranquil embrace of a glade nestled at the edge of the forest, Evelyn Stone stood in the yard of her cabin, her gaze fixed upon the garden that James had tended with such care. It was a sanctuary of blossoms and blooms—a testament to his love for nature and the quiet beauty of their mountain home. But since his passing, the garden had become a silent witness to its once vibrant colors muted by time and sorrow. A once-charming pond was overgrown with weeds, and its waters stagnant.

Clasping her well-worn locket, its silver surface worn smooth, Evelyn felt the weight of James's memory pressed against her heart—a talisman of love and loss.

Evelyn turned away from the neglected garden and ventured into the forest. Sunlight, barely piercing the dense foliage, cast a melancholic glow upon its floor where ferns unfurled like mournful tendrils and wildflowers drooped in the still air. Her footsteps were weighed down by the burden of sorrow—a yearning for solace, for understanding, for a glimpse of the beauty that had once filled her world.

Lost in painful memories, Evelyn scarcely noticed the passage of time. Each twist and turn of the meandering path revealed new reminders of the life she had lost—a hidden glade where a crystal-clear stream whispered of forgotten dreams, a moss-covered log where a family of rabbits played amidst the shadows, a grove of ancient oaks whose branches seemed to reach out in silent supplication to the heavens.

And then, just as the sun began its slow descent toward the horizon, Evelyn came upon a clearing—a place of haunting beauty. The air was heavy with the echo of birdcalls, a mournful symphony that filled the forest with a sense of longing. In the center of the clearing stood a solitary oak, its gnarled branches stretching towards the sky like fingers grasping for a fleeting glimpse of hope.

Here, amidst the melancholy beauty of the forest, Evelyn felt a sense of resignation wash over her—a quiet acceptance that, no matter what trials lay ahead, she would always be haunted by the specter of her fallen James. As she stood beneath the ancient oak, its branches swaying gently in the breeze, Evelyn felt the weight of her sorrow press down upon her like a leaden shroud, suffocating the flicker of hope that struggled to ignite within her.

Evelyn ventured further into the garden; her footsteps soft upon the earth. She found herself drawn to a fragrant flower bed nestled amidst the tangled greenery. The blooms fluttered in the light wind, their petals kissed by flickering sun rays, filling the air with a heady perfume that stirred memories long buried beneath the weight of grief.

With trembling fingers, Evelyn reached out to one of the flowers, its velvety petals soft beneath her touch. She brought the blossom to her nose and inhaled its sweet scent. A kaleidoscope of images and sensations transported her back to the day she had first met James.

She remembered the warmth of the sun on her skin, the laughter that had danced upon the breeze, and the sight of James standing before her, his eyes sparkling with mischief and delight. It was a day filled with the promise of new beginnings and the thrill of unexpected encounters.

Evelyn stood amidst the fragrant blooms; her sorrow deepened by the bittersweet ache of remembrance.

A figure emerged from the shadows—solitary and clad in robes of deepest green, their face obscured by the veil of time.

"The Celestial Bloom," the figure murmured, their voice like the rustle of leaves in the breeze. "It is a rare and wondrous flower, cherished by all who behold it."

Startled, Evelyn turned to face the speaker; her eyes widening in astonishment. She beheld the enigmatic being before her, cloaked in the mantle of ages, their presence suffused with otherworldly grace.

"The Celestial Bloom?" Evelyn echoed—her voice barely more than a whisper. "I have never heard of such a flower."

They nodded, a hint of sadness shadowing their features. "Few have, my dear," they replied. "Cherish it for its fragile beauty."

Collection 16

As Evelyn gazed at the flower, its petals wilted. She spread her fingers, and the petals fell to the forest floor.

"I am the Timekeeper ... and this is my garden." They spread their arms wide, beckoning Evelyn to take in the vast patches of color and shadow bound by the clumped red dirt path at their feet. "Follow me, Evelyn Stone."

The two traversed a deeply shadowed hollow punctuated with speckles of sunlight illuminating clusters of pale pink and white.

Evelyn noticed a new fragrance in the air—a rich, sweet scent that enveloped her in its embrace. Turning to the Timekeeper, she saw them nod in acknowledgment.

"Within the darkness, the sun's warmth reveals the power of jasmine," their voice evidencing a certain steeliness. "It is a flower of tenacity, of strength, of moving forward."

Evelyn closed her eyes, breathing in the heady scent of jasmine, drinking in its intoxicating fragrance. A sense of clarity washed over her—a realization that while the past was filled with passions dulled by longing, the future might promise new beginnings.

Opening her eyes, Evelyn met the Timekeeper's gaze with newfound determination.

The Timekeeper smiled a knowing smile that seemed to hold the wisdom of the ages. "We have not finished," they said, their voice gentle yet firm.

As they rounded a bend in the path, Evelyn's breath caught in her throat. Stretching out before her was a garden unlike any she had ever seen—a riotous tapestry of colors and textures that danced and shimmered in the sunlight.

There were flowers of every hue imaginable—roses and lilies, daisies and tulips, their petals unfolding like delicate works of art. Evelyn bent to caress each flower. Memories of James flooded her mind—the way he had given her roses on their first date, the lilies he had planted in their garden, the tulips that had bloomed in the spring, and the daisies they had picked and plucked on lazy summer afternoons.

The air was filled with the sound of trickling water, the gentle rustle of leaves, and the melodious song of birds in flight.

Before her stretched a tranquil pond, its surface shimmering in the dappled sunlight like liquid glass.

Metamorphosis

Drawn by an unseen force, Evelyn knelt beside the pond. She trailed one hand lightly across the surface of the water, the other cradling the open locket.

The Timekeeper stood behind Evelyn, a silent presence that filled her with a sense of peace. With a solemn gesture, they unclasped the delicate chain of the locket. "The time has come," they whispered.

Evelyn gently extended her hand and spread her fingers. With a hushed splash, a semicircle of ripples unfurled. Slowly sinking into the tranquil depths, James's face smiled up to her.

As the Timekeeper dissolved into the shadows, Evelyn's gaze shifted back to the pond. A smile tugged at her lips.

A flight of dragonflies ... their iridescent wings caught the sunlight and weaved a dance above the reflection of her quaint wooden cabin nestled amidst blossoming trees. Its warm and honey-colored walls embraced the dusk's golden hue. From the chimney, a wisp of smoke curled lazily into the evening sky.

One Small Act

by **Lynn Taylor**

"Do you have your homework?"
"Yep!"
"Lunch money?"
"Mom, how many times are you going to ask me?" Kaya shoots me a disgusted look. It's her third week of school after winter break, and she's already annoyed with me.

"Let them handle it," my husband says. "Builds responsibility." But he leaves for work before Blake and Kaya are even up.

I went through the same routine with Blake an hour ago. He is three years older and doesn't seem to need as much reminding, but I still ask to be sure he has everything. Soccer jersey, field trip permission slip. Homework, again.

Kaya crams her homework into her backpack, then slings a strap over her shoulder. I wait with her on the front porch until the school bus pulls up, then pretend to straighten the wicker furniture until she's safely on the bus and it lumbers down the street toward the school.

I breathe in the possibilities of a day alone, imagining myself on a tropical beach, my body soothed by the sun like the strokes of an expert masseuse. More likely, I will attempt to eke out a few paragraphs of my novel. The truth is, I've barely written a word in months. I open the document and reread the first chapter, the words becoming less familiar to me each time I do.

I used to get through writing blocks by wasting time online, reading celebrity gossip, what novels made the *New York Times* bestseller list, which movies had the highest percentages on Rotten Tomatoes. Now all I find are wars, political divides, the weather disturbances of a warming planet,

Metamorphosis

children at the border, racial injustice. It's hard to focus on a fictional world when there are so many real things to think about.

I glance at my phone. I've wasted an hour ruminating instead of writing. Today's my day to volunteer at the food pantry, so I close my laptop and head downtown.

Marian is there when I arrive, her gray hair wound in a pink scrunchie. She empties boxes of canned soups and vegetables and places them in neat rows on the shelf. We're the only food pantry for twenty miles, and we've been even busier lately due to rising food costs and cuts to the SNAP program.

"Just us today," she says. "Jo's daughter went into labor. They're headed to the hospital now."

"No problem," I say and look at the clock, a simple black schoolhouse model that's been on that wall for decades. Forty-five minutes until we open, but we've done this by ourselves plenty of times before.

Marian points to a large box filled with cereal and pasta. "We've got time to make up some bags. That'll help move things along. How're the kids?" She stands still, waiting for my reply.

Marian is always in constant motion, but she gives her full attention when she's talking to someone. There's never any doubt that she's really listening.

"The kids are good. Back in school." I start filling the paper bags with canned beans and jars of tomato sauce with meat or plain for vegetarians, then add boxes of spaghetti, cereal, and day-old bread donated by the bakery on Main Street.

We fill two dozen bags, then stack the empty boxes by the back door.

Marian pours two cups of iced tea from a large yellow thermos and hands me one. "And how're you?"

"Busy with the kids. And the new novel." I slip that in like it's actually true.

"How's that book coming along?" She sips her tea, not taking her dark eyes off me.

I start to say fine but can't get the word out. "It's not," I tell her, surprising myself. What I don't say is my mind is so full of the world that it's impossible to write.

The room is quiet except for the steady ticking of the old clock.

But Marian doesn't check the time. She looks at me, like we've got all day, like there won't soon be parents lined up needing to feed their children and seniors on such limited budgets they have to choose between

Collection 16

groceries or medication. She pulls the full-length apron she wears to protect her clothes over her head. "Why is that?"

She won't let up until I tell her. "There's too much to worry about. My kids, other people's kids, the country, the planet. There's no room in my head for anything else."

It's five to ten. I put my apron on too. I'm embarrassed at my petty problems. In a few minutes, the pantry will soon fill with women holding babies, men who look embarrassed like they came to the wrong place, elderly couples needing help carrying their bags to their cars.

"It takes courage to live in these times, but like they tell you on an airplane—put your own oxygen mask on first. You've got to take care of yourself before you can be of help to anyone else. That one small act can save two lives instead of one."

It's ten o'clock. I give Marian a hug and rush to unlock the door, wiping away tears. She always knows exactly the right thing to say. A line has already formed outside. I tell everyone to come in and have a seat in the lobby where Marian has laid out paper cups of iced tea and her homemade chocolate chip cookies. I talk to each family to assess their specific needs, hoping we can fulfill them, no matter how temporarily. Marian takes care of the paperwork. I give each family a bag of food that will hopefully last a week. It's not much, but it's something.

The next morning, I clean up the breakfast dishes and wait for Kaya to finish getting ready for school.

"Almost done," she says.

I lean against the counter, drinking my coffee.

"Aren't you gonna ask if I have my homework and my lunch money?"

"Nope. You've got this."

She stops lacing her sneakers and looks up at me, her face a question mark. "Where'd my mom go?"

I wrap my arms around her, and she lets me. I hold the door open and follow her out to the front porch.

After the school bus drives away, I go inside to refill my coffee. I think of Marian's analogy. How one small act, one small productive step forward could save two lives. In that context, it's not selfish to consider your own needs. I think of my writing and how many times it has rescued me.

I go inside and bring my laptop out to the porch and settle into one of the wicker chairs. The morning sun filters through the trees. Two blue jays squabble on a low branch. I open the laptop and click on the document that contains my novel. As I read, I remember why I started this particular story in the first place—to try and make sense of the confusion going on in the world. I start to type, and I keep going.

Be Hopeful What You Wish For

by Ed N. White

A high-pitched, strident voice crackled through the cone-shaped speaker fastened to the concrete block wall in the bakery warehouse, interrupting the whimsical thoughts and quiet humming of the young girl sweeping the floor. She was a petite girl with unsettled mousey hair, wearing ragged bib overalls and a hand-me-down, faded pink T-shirt with a fairy princess logo.

"Mummy says you need to hurry because the Rinaldis are waiting for a delivery, so shake it up, sweet cheeks, chop-chop." This sarcastic voice broke through the sweeper's dreams and returned her to the harsh reality of her everyday world.

She sighed and muttered to the muted speaker, "Of course, Ann-ass-stasia, your mummy's wish is my command." After pushing the Green Kleen sweeping compound into a small pile by the door, she grasped the broom in two hands and twirled about the floor, dancing with her dreams and humming a song she had written last night while tucked under the bedcovers using the Evernote phone app. She set the broom in the corner, buckled on her bike helmet, placed the cinnamon-smelling wrapped package in the wicker basket attached to the handlebars, and swiftly pedaled to the Rinaldi home in the upscale Maplelawn section of town, hoping, hoping, hoping Tommy Rinaldi would answer the door when she rang. His mother received the package, but Cindie saw Tommy throwing a tennis ball for his dog in the backyard. Her heart skipped and danced.

Metamorphosis

She went to bed that night whispering, "Someday, someday..." and drifted to sleep with pleasant dreams of musical stardom and Tommy Rinaldi tripping lightly through her mind.

Cindie's life was under constant harassment from her two older stepsisters—Anna, mentioned earlier, and the mean one everyone called Grizzly, of course, not to Griselda's face. That would provoke a torrent of abuse. It was bad enough with the anxiety of the Spring Ball coming up at Tisdale High School next month and the stepsisters vying for attention and nomination as the Spring Queen. Everyone expected the handsome Tommy Rinaldi to be the king. Cindie had no gown, no date, and no chance. She hoped, at best, to attend and sit in the shadows, listening to the music. She could always dance in her head.

When she discovered TikTok, the videos on the social media giant inspired her. She practiced her latest song and dance routine after the bakery closed and her stepsisters had gone home with Mummy to their cozy house in the burbs. Cindie had a small room over the bakery and relished the solitude when the bakery became her castle. She cleaned and polished the stainless steel equipment, coolers, and stoves as if they were medieval armor worn by her knight, who would come astride a great white horse to rescue her and carry her to a better world away from the constant harangue of her stepsisters. She sang and danced through her chores, hoping, hoping, hoping.

After weeks of solitary practice, Cindie was ready. She had rehearsed her song so often that the lyrics had pasted on to her brain. She danced so much that her worn Converse Chucks exfoliated, and the rubber peeled away from the fabric. But now she was ready and propped her phone on a stack of pallets in the warehouse, turned on all the overhead lights, grabbed the push broom, hit the record button to start the video, and began the performance of her young life—hoping, hoping, hoping.

Team captain Tommy Rinaldi strode into the locker room, his metal baseball cleats clicking on the concrete. After hitting a two-run homer over the left-field fence at the bottom of the ninth to win the game, his teammates cheered him from the field into the locker room. Coach Nunes shook his hand and clapped him on the back. When the carousing ended, Eddie

Collection 16

Nolan, sitting next to him on the locker bench, said, "So, Tommy, who's your date for the Spring Ball?"

"Someone special. I don't know her name yet, but she looks kinda familiar. I can't place her though." Tommy looked wistfully across the room as he wrapped a towel around himself and headed for the showers. "But I'll search until I find her."

"What? She's special, but you don't know her name?" Eddie was following and dodged the towel Butch Jordan snapped at him as he passed. "How do you expect to find her? That's weird."

They stood in the showers, yelling past the steam and pouring water. Tommy said, "Yeah, I saw her singing and dancing on TikTok. She calls herself 'Sugar Bun.'"

"You're kidding."

"No, really, she's this hot girl who dances with a broom and has a great song, 'Dancing, With My Dreams.' She wrote it herself. Man, she's blowing up TikTok with nearly a million likes. Maybe more than that today."

"Whoa, how are you gonna find her in cyberspace?"

"I'm sure I've seen her around here. I know I have."

"You mean here, in town?"

"Yeah, I'm sure of it. I need to remember where."

"Send me a link to her video."

Tommy chuckled and said, "I can do better than that."

When they returned to their lockers, Tommy grabbed his phone from the shelf. "Look, I have her video on my phone."

Eddie watched the video, his eyes squinting and his nose scrunching. "Yeah . . . she looks familiar. Man, she is hot. Whoa, you've gotta find her, then you can ditch what's her name."

"Yeah, Anna. Her complete name is Anastasia. Can you imagine? She thinks she's some princess or something, and she's hoping to be the Spring Ball Queen."

"Oh, yeah, and her mean sister, you know Gin . . . Grinn . . . something like that."

"Yeah, Griselda, Tommy said. "She's nasty. She sometimes works at the bakery . . . Wait! That's it, Eddie. That's it!"

Eddie squinted and scrunched again. "What's it?"

Metamorphosis

"The bakery. The other girl, not Anna, not Grizzly. The younger one who works in the kitchen and warehouse. I don't know her name. She delivered bread to my house last week."

"What? She's a bakery girl? Are you kidding?"

"No, I'm going there now. I'll invite her to the dance."

"Go for it." Eddie gave Tommy a friendly shove. "You got this, dude."

On the dance night, Tommy picked her up in his new Dodge Charger R/T pulled by an eager 375 horses, and like all beautiful fairy tales this night ended happily ever after. Tommy became the King of the Spring Ball, and Anastasia barely secured enough votes to be crowned the queen.

But, breaking with the long-standing school tradition, Tommy Rinaldi's date was not the queen but rather the TikTok sensation Sugar Bun, wearing an eye-popping, sequin-laden Glam-Trend gown made expressly for her by Jovani in New York, purchased with the advance provided by Sony Records when they signed her to a one-year contract with extensions. She ditched her well-worn Chucks for the glove-soft fawn-colored heels custom-made by Girotti in Italy—shoes that made her tall enough to rest her head against Tommy's broad shoulder as they danced the night away under the dagger-like stares of her seething stepsisters.

Sometimes, a dream will come true. And like the caterpillar, it morphs into a colorful butterfly with gossamer wings. So, too, can a humble bakery girl become a star internet music sensation and, eventually, the wife of the former Spring Ball King—the man who became the youngest person ever elected governor of this fine state. During his gubernatorial acceptance speech, he introduced his wife and mother of their children—the Grammy award-winning singer internationally celebrated as Sugar Bun.

POETRY

Madeira Beach Urchin

by Rose Angelina Baptista

The urge to walk
barefoot ashore
during winter
on Madeira Beach . . .

Ah, a sweet encounter! Seeing
a sea urchin polished
by sand and sound alarmed
my heart, both of us from parted

islands in solitary
spiky armored worlds.
Slowly moving
breathing without lungs,

standing with no limbs
boneless tonsured souls
desire less of wings.
Our ineffable metamorphosis

from eggs to larvae,
he acquired one sole eye,
and soon eventually perishing
in pure symmetry of a circle

cracked in the ruins

Metamorphosis

of a fairytale castle
which will always exude
serene composure.

Was that pretty urchin dead or alive?
He made me go beyond
becoming, so now I am awakened
stirred by a purple sea of the South Coast.

For the Better

by Nancy Lee Bethea

I am cells and sinew,
A body living
As daughter and sister, wife and mother.
I grow.

I am feeling and emotion,
A heart palpitating
Crushes and commitments, preferences and beliefs.
I love.

I am facts and opinions,
A mind imagining
Characters and plots, stories and songs.
I create.

I am prayers and praise
A soul worshipping
A Center other than myself.
I relent.

What I once was
Fell away.

What I will be
Is part of an array
Of failures and victories,

Metamorphosis

Sorrows and joys.

But I know
I am changed for the better.

Did I Know Love?

by Deb Crutcher

Who looks outside, dreams
Who looks inside, awakes
      Carl Jung

Did a caterpillar know
she would soon be an
emerging butterfly
flitting, floating from
nectar to sweeter nectar?

Did a thorny rose know
its tiny velvet bud would
burst with nature's beauty
and pure essence
until it bloomed?

Did a sculptor know
his hardened hands
and diligent laboring
would reveal a masterpiece
until he shaped his stone?

Did I know that
decades of internal conflict
failed attempts at chasing love
striving for perfection

Metamorphosis

would bring no lasting peace?

Did I know love, self-love
until I journeyed within
witnessed my truest heart
unfurled my wings
and just let go?

Mammatus Theatre

by Madeline Izzo

If I were to write about this, it would be in the form of a play. It comes to me in flashes, static scenes like a series of tableaux. Mammatus clouds pouch overhead—drooping, ominous, gray—casting everything below in a sick yellow light, or the green you see before a tornado pokes its witchy finger down.

I made a theater out of a shoebox once—puppets cut out of red construction paper, outlined in black Sharpie, glued on skewers—my daughter loved it. This play might use puppets too—marionettes made from cardstock with grommets for joints, or shadow puppets perhaps—or maybe dancers—Kabuki dancers or dancers from India or Thailand—I have not decided yet.

Act I. I am subject and object
I lie in my johnny in the radiologist's office. The doctor takes a sonogram. "Yep, that's cancer," she says. I curl onto my side and cry softly. She snaps a metal clip into my left breast, close to the nipple—the offending duct. I am a marionette with disconnected joints—jerky, stumbling, graceless. I call my husband, do not cry while I am telling him.

Act II. Preparation
A whirlwind of phone calls, doctors' appointments, charts, handouts, tests. I put off calling my daughter in Paris because she will want to come home, but I want her to finish her semester.

Last hurrah: I slip on a form-fitting red dress with a lowcut neckline. We go out to dinner at The Casbah in Shadyside. Moon and stars through a tiny window, white sculptures of nude torsos on the walls, topiary in a vase. I feel truncated, raw.

Act III. Mastectomy

Lying naked under a blanket in the operating room, I ask the knife to be kind, to find its mark, to excise the bad, and save what it can. I emerge in a fog.

Act IV. Recovery

Wound care, my scar, a handout full of exercises. My mother travels from Rhode Island to Pittsburgh to clean my drains. I set my father to work, fixing that place outside the door to our deck where the rain pools and wicks up the wood, blistering the paint.

Exercises, therapy, posters of green lymph nodes on the walls—the system I never knew I had. Good news: they got it all; I do not need chemo or radiation. One in eight, I am a statistic!

Act V. Reconstruction

A new breast, a new life—I do not know what this will look like yet.

First, visits to pump up the expander. My pectoral muscle is stretched to form a sling that will cradle the implant. Second, another surgery: my new breast is now silicone.

Scenes come to me in flashes: doctors in a chorus line—smiling, dancing, kicking high; helping hands reaching out, unexpected visits, my calico in a corner; smiling faces of family around a table piled with protein for muscle growth—beef, pork, custard!

Props: the omnipresence of technology and medical devices, barbells and stretchy bands, cards, books, gifts, a subscription to *People* magazine, my smartphone—where would I be without solitaire? A squishy, red heart pillow from a friend who had a mastectomy before me. I fit this into my armpit so I can sleep at night.

Final scene: Me, naked, dancing on the stage, fingers splayed like a Balinese dancer, one leg bent, the other in the air, toes stretched back—heel, arch, ball.

Curtain down, lights out while I hold the final pose—torso with a hole in my chest, my mouth stretched wide in a grimace more than a smile.

I am me but not me. Shattered and rebuilt. I am a chorus of frogs, singing at the top of my lungs.

Transmutation

by **Denis O. Keeran**

My gaze surveys a dusty, arid plot.
It seems vitality has been forgot!
But hope exists if measures taken soon
And abiotic factors keep in tune.

The soil is tilled, nutrients blended in.
Plants are thriving inviting more to win!
A transformation taking place at last!
The lifeless wasteland, now a place of past.

My garden spreads, a potpourri of Life!
To keep it rich and minimize the strife
I must observe, keep up with what they need.
If all goes well, they will produce some seed!

This barren desert, once devoid of green
Has now transformed to lushness never seen!

Manufacturing a Persona

by Linda Kraus

A woman has learned how to adapt,
to change her persona to catch a man.
To land a trout, she carefully selects
the proper fly, baits her hook, and
reels him in expertly.
Her quirks, the tropes that once
attracted him and made her unique,
are slowly chipped away, a
purposeful accommodation to his
criticisms and tastes.
Conservative clothing, suitable
for a Sunday school teacher, replaces
her once-praised Bohemian style.
Exquisite rings and bracelets
are swapped for her signature funk.
She no longer peppers her speech
with profanity; she's a cleaned-up,
safe-to-exhibit-in-public paragon,
suitable to be invited
to tea with the Queen.
When her relationship eventually fizzles,
she has not only lost a lover,
but her former self,
never to be reclaimed.

Metamorphosis

by **Donna Parrey**

A theme,
a single word,
like a solitary cell,
will divide, then divide again.
Then will multiply, and multiply again.
You write with passion as your manuscript grows.

One day,
you allow it to rest,
cocooned, safe from further
meddling. Yet during this restful stage,
your manuscript is not dormant. It is alive and you
continue to shape and feed it—in your mind, your heart, your soul.

The season beckons
and tells you that it is time.
You approach the manuscript
nested in its cocoon and feel it pulse.
Its shell splits and exposes the pages within.
Through osmosis, you have added wings to your story.

During the time needed to rest,
your story grew and generated complexity.
Now, the shell falls away, and your book shakes out its
gossamer wings. The colors please you. Its life leaves you breathless.
You step away and allow it to take flight, hoping its beauty will stun
the world.

The metamorphosis from a single-celled theme to your book is complete.

Hummingbird

by David Spiegel

Your cheek is damp and icy to my touch,
like my father's when they found him in the lake.
I trace familiar curves with desperate fingers
and beg the brutal cold to take me too,
numb my senses, curdle my blood, clog my heart,
that I can join you in your final passage
as we shared all else in life.

The mortuary room is empty but for us,
nothing to disturb my private grieving,
so a quiet thrumming at my ear, a low oboe trill,
startles me. A hummingbird is in the room, confined
like you, inside. It floats before me, wings sculling
fiercely the frigid air, then darts away, a blur,
to perch somewhere above.

I don't believe in the transmigration of souls,
or that birds have true symbolic meanings,
but the hummingbird reminds me of the day
your mother died, when you remarked you'd never
seen one, and one flew up and hovered. And when
we told a friend; she said hummingbirds are
departed loved ones come to visit.

I don't believe, either, in the bodily chakras of Indian
faiths, swirling pools of energy and memories. And

Collection 16

yours would be empty now anyway, their contents freed
and sighed out. Yet when I press my lips to your forehead,
chakra gateway to the past and future, I taste the chilled
champagne we drank at our wedding and feel our hot
impatience to entwine our destinies.

What I do believe in is the vast sprawl of the universe,
its sudden birth and headlong rush to death,
and the miracle that, at an insignificant place in those
dark reaches, conditions came together to create us.
That, against incredible odds, we passed here briefly,
and found each other, and experienced the joy of love.
And I fill with gratitude.

I say that to you now, my face as wet as yours,
our last pillow-talk in a journey measured out in them.
I smooth a loose lock of your hair, adjust your collar,
touch my fingers to my lips and then to yours.
As I leave, I pause and hold the door open.
The hummingbird flits down from its perch
and comes out with me.

I-4 West

by K.M. Stull

Welcome to a life lived backwards
remember when, remember when
your soft baby head in the palm of my hand
your first toddler sentences I wrote down
amazed by the brilliance of your brand-new mind

Goodbye forever, you sent this morning
because that's the way we talk to each other
a quip, a laugh, a roll of the eyes

Slowly those paths in the yellow wood
stop diverging
the cicadas whine from the canopy
the leaves crackle gently under foot
I glimpse you through the trees
clearing away brambles and clambering over rocks
the weather is wilder there
sometimes the nights are darker
I remember that too

A Loss for Words

by Sylvia Whitman

It began on the phone, with *Fine*,
and my father in the background, *You are not fine. You are driving me crazy.*

For once, she did not snap back.
In person we found she had less and less to say,

so we asked doctors for words of explanation.
Aphasia, they said, which described but did not elucidate.

It sounded like one of the flowers in her gardens.
She loved to plant bulbs, take planes, drink wine, tell stories.

I have no words for the feeling
the first time I hugged my mother and said, *Goodbye, Mom,*

and she said, *Goodbye, Mom.*
Even that was better than now,

my father dead and from my mother nothing.
Just silence.

Coquina Beach
by **Robin Zabel**

I wander the rough shore
balancing carefully on
Coquina rocks that
capture the gurgling tide
in pockets of weathered
sand and shell.

My life too is pockmarked
by changing tides of
death and transition,
loss and expansion,
high desert turquoise skies
to the rhythmic breath of the ocean.

All is new, reborn,
ready to be molded into
a different form, seamless, smooth
without jagged edges.
Unresisting, I open my arms wide
to embrace the brine-scented dawn.

NEXTGEN WRITERS

AGES 9 - 17

Childhood

by **Perla Anderson**

As I sink into my favorite armchair
By the fireplace
I reflect upon my life
I know that I have changed over time
But how?
As a young girl
I was carefree and full of joy
A sense of wonder filled me
The kitchen rug was my magic carpet
And the dining table, a pirate ship.
The days were long and untouched
By care or worry
It was a time of innocence.
Then, as I got older
I was taught many things
Some by teachers
Others by parents and friends.
The days were shorter
My life and mind grew fuller.
Joy is now a visitor
Instead of a companion.
Is this knowledge I have gained
Or did I know something more in childhood?
Have I traded wonder for knowing
And joy and freedom for a schedule?
Is this what growing up has to be?

Metamorphosis

I ponder this question as I sip my tea.
I stand up from my chair
And declare that it is, indeed, a choice.
Today, I will find the extraordinary
In the ordinary
And throw off the chains of time.
I hear the impatient ocean waves crash
As I enter my dining room
There my ship awaits.

Saul to Paul

by Jace Burke

Long ago, there was a man named Saul of Tarsus
He persecuted Christians yet to no catharsis
Breathing out murderous threats to the Lord's disciples
Going against the speech and rules in the Bible.

On his way to discredit and persecute in Damascus
He comes upon a glorious light, that named himself as Jesus
As quoted from the word Saul and his company were left speechless
After three days without eating or drinking, he was approached by Ananias.

The Lord still forgave him, and he was filled with the Holy Ghost
Now he started preaching and grew more powerful than most
Changing from Saul to Paul, erasing the past
Through Jesus Christ the King, he made his future last.

With spreading His word, the Church grew fast
Paul converted the Jews and Gentiles through his preaching
Making many new converts from his teaching
Showing the power of Jesus Christ through his speaking.

Even though he was persecuted for his belief and forced to suffer,
In the end it was him who didn't have hell, a fate worse than any other
Staying true to the Word until his end,
Rather than fighting back, he fell on his own sword to ascend.

Amen.

A Frog's Journey

by **Grayson Carpel**

I was sitting on a rock by a stream in the fog,
When I saw a bright, green tree frog.
Hopping around glistening in the sun.
The fog seemed to be on the run.

Running from the turtle, while trying to hurdle.
Hurdling over the log, while in the fog.
The frog got away and kept the turtle at bay.
The turtle missed his chance at getting his prey.

While chasing a fly, the frog had a hunch.
He hopped on a log and saw a girl frog.
In search of a mate, the frog thought it must be fate.
The frogs frolicked joyfully as they hopped in the stream playfully.

The girl frog in the sun's glow, she lays her eggs in the water below.
Tadpoles wiggle in delight. It was a beautiful sight.
As the cycle spins, from eggs to tadpoles,
That's where life begins.

The frog then makes a new journey, hopefully bright,
Just as this froggy's delight.

Through the Seasons
by Ebelle Imani Creve-Coeur

Out of winter's cocoon,
Spring blossoms emerge
Signaling life's
Metamorphosis
Hope buds in joyful colors
Fresh beginnings bloom
Once again
Nature paints its perfect picture.
Soon, summer's sunlight
Beams and frolics
Over the beauty
Of last spring
Giving a warm embrace,
Dreams take flight.
Autumn comes around,
With its golden flare,
Leaves whisper
Throughout the meadows.
Golden flakes cloak the earth.
Wrapped in December's blanket,
The cocoon closes,
Once again.

Nature's Gift

by **Sydney Crane**

The cool, dry capsule sits in the shadow,
Saving the emergent life from danger,
Encasing a tiny spirit aglow,
Providing the comfort of a manger.
Then, suddenly, He says, "Let there be light."
And a peculiar radiance rose,
From this day, its metamorphosis goes.

Cycles of sunlight and heatwaves forge on,
Small embryo, supplied with nutrients,
A protective covering holding strong,
Like a cell membrane and a nucleus,
Then, He established Heaven and Earth,
And the membrane cracked, opened, and led way,
Roots poke and prod for water like crochet.

The plant weaves its roots farther underground,
Giving it stability in dry land,
Mother Earth cheers on her new life compound,
Germination produces a stem strand,
Then, He generates the green and the blue,
Clouds cry their droplets of gifts of water,
The seedling springs up like a true daughter.

Expanding, taking up space like matter,
Small protrusions with pores on the surface,

Collection 16

Leaves go across like rungs on a ladder,
Securing the sun's power for service,
Then, He separated day from the night,
Giving the plant rest from the sun's strong beams,
So it retains its water while it dreams.

One morning, dew drenching its leaves and stem,
The plant presented a gift to the world,
Wrapped in a delicate flower, a gem,
Lay peaceful when suddenly something whirled,
He created the birds that rule the sky,
And now they pecked at the pollen inside,
Soaring through clouds, they spread the pollen wide.

Petals folding back, its color fleeting,
Although, at its core, the flower still grew,
This plant was not done, its heart still beating,
A white sphere of sweetness came into view,
Then, He placed on Earth humans and fauna,
Who witnessed the strawberry swell and blush,
And yearned as the fruit became red and lush.

Why must it take so long? The humans thought,
Guarding the plant from predators each day,
Nights miserably long, days restlessly hot,
The strawberry seemed to be a prized prey,
Then, He set up the Sabbath day of rest,
And it came time to harvest the plant's prize,
The humans gave thanks and lauded the skies.

My Basketball Career
A creative nonfiction

by Reece Hemmett

I started playing basketball at a young age on a mini hoop in my basement. I can remember listening to Stephen Curry's inspirational music videos while playing. My family lived in Vermont, so I could only play basketball for half the year because of the snow. But during March Madness, I would jump on the snow banks and to the hoop for the dunk while imagining I was on the Gonzaga Bulldogs team.

    I tried out for my first basketball team in third grade. It was a pretty good fourth-grade-travel team, and I was a year younger than everyone. I was not great at basketball. When I tried out, I could tell that I was not the best. Afterwards, I nervously waited for a few days to find out if I made the team or not. My dad told me I had made it and that the coach said it wasn't because of my skill but how hard I worked. That season I had to learn the game, so I sat on the bench as our team made it all the way to winning the regional championship. However, I got much better in my fundamentals and overall skills and had lots of fun hanging out with the team. After that season, I worked almost every day in the offseason and got much better at basketball.

    The next year, I went to tryouts confident and with more skill than the previous year. I made the fourth- and fifth-grade teams. I was the star player on the fourth-grade team and a starter on both teams. That year was a ton of fun because I saw the floor ten times as much as the previous year and got to be around kids my age and older.

    When our family moved to Florida, it helped my basketball game tremendously. I could now play year-round and had 24/7 access to an indoor basketball court in our community. My first season in Florida, I was with a travel team called For the Love. I made it as a fifth grader, although it was a sixth-grade team. I was coached by the sheriff who also coached flag football earlier in the year. I started the year as the shooting guard because I was the best shooter on the team.

Collection 16

We started playing in a rec league against high schoolers where we learned our plays and got ready to play in the real games for the upcoming tournaments. That year was really all about finding out what kind of player I was. I went into the first game ready. I was the leading scorer that year mostly because of how good of a shooter I was; at that level, not many players could guard the three-point shot.

I also played baseball, and my elbow had been hurting throughout the season, so I went to get an X-ray. It showed that I had a small fracture and that I had to wear a cast for four months. This meant I had to sit out the biggest tournament of the season. I was super sad about it but used this opportunity to work on my left hand, which was one of my biggest flaws. Every day I would practice shooting, layups, and cardio training in preparation for the next year.

Between seasons, I played for a private school called First Baptist Academy where I played with eighth graders as a sixth grader. In season, I was again the best shooter and now much better with my left hand. Although I was on the bench, I played decent minutes per game, and we ended up with only one loss that year and won the championship.

When I played on the seventh-grade For the Love team, two new kids took my starting spot. This team was much better than the last, and I saw much less playing time. We played in big tournaments against teams from other states and beat most of them. I had limited playing time, but I made the most out of it and made many threes along the way. In the national tournament, I led the team in points in the first game and scored well in the rest of the games. That whole season led up to the championship game where we won the game on the three pointer I made.

I just finished playing Junior Varsity (JV) for First Baptist Academy as a seventh grader, and I also started on the middle school team. I led the team in threes and was the only player on JV who got the green light to shoot whenever I wanted. On the middle school team, I was the second leading scorer, and we went undefeated for the first time in a long time. In the playoffs, I had seventeen points in the semifinals and fifteen in the finals which were both the team highs.

Going into this next For the Love season, I am fighting with other players for a starting spot. My basketball career so far is beyond what I had imagined was possible back when I was just a young kid dunking in the snow on Gonzaga.

The Seasonal Cycle

by McKayla R. Lindor

The snow is melting away
Everyone is coming out to play
The children are watching the flowers bloom
Before they stayed in their room
Waiting for it to get a little less cooler
Since Papa bores us with his bad humor
It's an easy day
Since Spring came and Winter went away
School's out for the summer
There was so much to discover
I challenged my brother to a race
I yelled across the block, "The first to win, gets their phone replaced"
Like dew on wet grass, summer left in a flash

Summer's heat faded away
Autumn was here to stay
After welcoming a subtle breeze
The leaves begin to fall from the trees
Red, yellow, and brown
I also watch those main colors fall to the ground
Winter is near
As the snow dances in the wind
I feel it twirling on my skin
My brother and I made snowballs big and round
I made my first cup of hot cocoa, Mama was proud
Puffer jackets, mittens, and ear muffs

Collection 16

The clothes I wore so Mama wouldn't make a fuss
The snow was fun
But it was really cold

Earth's Evolution

by **Hudson D. Lowe**

Nothing at first
It was desolate and frozen
Things started to heat up
Life was yet to be chosen
When it got too hot
It needed to cool down
And when others rammed into it
They should have slowed down
But a companion formed
Named Luna, or Moon
And I have no idea why
I feel change coming soon
I predicted it right
Just as I said
Now liquid created
But things are still dead
From the liquid that was formed
Which, unlike others, is water
Came an itty-bitty cell
Let's call it Life's Father
This cell multiplied
Creating other things too
Like plankton, bacteria
But that's only a few
Many, many eras later
After plants had been created
Dinosaurs roamed the Earth
But they were all decimated
After all of that had happened
And other animals came to be
Humans were born
The ones like you and me

An Ode to Motherhood

by **Madeline Pesi**

Like Nona, like mother, like daughter.

"You look so much like your mother!"

Recessive genes that seem to skip around, I see them branch out of me.

My grandmother's hang for crafting,
the spider's woven web,

The gold hoops that've been worn earlobe from earlobe,
the leaves that will always blossom into a peach.

Something built within my core,
the rings of my family tree wrapping around me.
My hands tunneling through the layers,

leaving a hollow in my memories of her,
but keeping her in my roots.

I am the culmination of the dialect,
slowly seeping out into my sappy words.
The confusion of a woodpecker striking its beak into our tree,
and leaving with a beak covered in sweetness and "Joan" and "Sally Ann"

These pieces of bark,
adhered since the age of a sapling,

Metamorphosis

soon beginning to extend into branches and flower
like the forests before

This growth was no small feat,
a process that was filled with much intended care.
Stakes jammed into the ground, decorated Easter cookies, simple cards, and visits up North.

Each visit they see:
A couple inches taller, an extra limb or two, new leaves to shed.
Young eyes blind to these personal seasons.
Young eyes desperate to go on a fruitless search,
to ignore the growing smile lines and crow's feet.

But a gratitude is had in these ridges,
they are the consequence of who I know now and who I hadn't.

They tell the same jokes,
I will form the same lines.
The caretaker becomes taken care of,
the cycle repeats.

Maybe my daughter will be just like me,
maybe she'll pick up my mother's habits.
Skipping over me, alternating revolutions.

Our tree adds another ring.

A Caterpillar to a Butterfly

by **Zayba Zafar**

A caterpillar is born
The process isn't always steady
But there is no rose without a thorn
When the cocoon hatches
A butterfly is ready

Now a butterfly
Oh so pretty
How will it fly?
It's so witty
Alone in the sky
What a pity

It's so new to this
Just hatched
Into an abyss
Where's the rest of the batch?

What's that?
Another butterfly?
Not alone off the bat?
It can fly!

Its wings flutter

Metamorphosis

The other butterfly is blue
Its wings are just like butter
While the new one just came out of a cocoon
The new butterfly stutters
How will it have a clue?

Our Contributors

Rose Angelina Baptista

Rose Angelina is a Brazilian American writer residing in Central Florida. Her poetry has been featured in *The Wallace Stevens Journal*, *LitBreak*, and *Gávea-Brown*.

Harry T. Barnes

Harry is author of *Condo Capers Mysteries*, the historical fiction series *Over the Barnes Bridge*, and numerous short stories and poems.

Nancy Lee Bethea

Nancy is a professional writer and educator from Northeast Florida. She was published in last year's Collection and she was an RPLA finalist.

P. K. Brent

P.K. enjoys writing fantasy, gothic, and sometimes literary fiction.

Metamorphosis

Barbara A. Busenbark

Barbara is an award-winning artist and author of *Uncharted: A widow's journey back to life and love cruising the Intracoastal Waterway.*

Adeline Carson

Adeline was born in Glendale, California. She is currently studying to become a film archivist. She lives with her family in Ocoee, Florida.

Scott Corey

Scott is the award-winning author of *Whistling for Hippos* and *Elephants in Paris*. He spends his time in St. Augustine, Kansas City, and Europe.

Deb Crutcher

Deb is a member of Winter Haven Writers group and has been published in anthologies, brochures, newsletters. *Living on the Edge* is her poetry collection.

Cheryl M. Dougherty

Cheryl is a retired educator from New Smyrna Beach, Florida, pursuing a lifelong dream of writing. This is her third published work.

Bob Ellis

Bob is a retired financial services executive. He has lived and worked on three continents and swum in all the oceans of the world.

Michael Farrell

Michael was captivated by stories of all different forms as a child. Now he aspires to master the connection between writer and reader.

Jim R. Garrison

Jim has written three published novels. He is a member of the Manatee Writers Group. He favors novels, short stories, and poetry.

Metamorphosis

Tilly Grey

Tilly was born in New York City, worked as a newspaper reporter, and a teacher. She had four children, including a boy with Down syndrome.

John Hope

John is an award-winning short-story, middle-grade, young-adult, science-fiction, fantasy, and historical fiction writer. He loves traveling and long-distance running.

Madeline Izzo

Madeline runs a flower farm in Pittsburgh where she writes and contemplates the universe.

Kelly Karsner-Clarke

Kelly lives in suburban Fort Lauderdale with her husband, children, and too many houseplants and pets.

Collection 16

Denis O. Keeran

Denis is a poet and singer/songwriter. He retired from teaching science and lives with his muse, Cathy, and their two rescue cats in Maitland.

Michele Verbitski Knudsen

Michele grew up in New Jersey but Florida's west coast captured her heart. Michele has a romantic mystery series in the works.

Linda Kraus

Linda is a professor of literature and cinema studies. She has published *Popcorn Icons and Other Poems Celebrating Movies* and *Listening to the Silence*.

Anthony Malone

Anthony's writing has appeared in Collections 13 &14 and he was an RPLA medalist. He worked as an Editorial Artist but now creates images with words.

Metamorphosis

Meredith Martin

Meredith lives in Dunnellon, Florida, with her dog Mandy and cat Cali. When not reading, she likes to photograph sunsets and clouds and to walk with Mandy.

Phyllis McKinley

This marks Phyllis's eleventh contribution to the Collection series. She has authored five books, many published pieces, and received multiple awards.

George August Meier

George's stories have appeared in many literary journals. He belongs to Florida Writers Association and Daytona Fiction Writers. He resides in Wilbur-By-The-Sea, Florida.

Joanna Michaels

Joanna's work has appeared in *Chicken Soup for the Soul*, *CafeLit*, *Drunk Monkeys*, and other publications. She earned her MFA at Queens University of Charlotte.

Micki Berthelot Morency

Micki is a Haitian American author who lives in St. Petersburg, Florida. *The Island Sisters* is her debut novel.

Mark H. Newhouse

Mark's *The Devil's Bookkeepers* won RPLA's Book of the Year and CIBA Grand Prize Fiction Series. His latest is *The Defenders of Monstrovia* podcast mystery series.

Donna Parrey

Donna is an experienced business writer, researcher, and editor. She's authored articles, essays, poetry, and children's books and continues to explore new writing horizons.

David Pearce

Traumatized by *Willy Wonka and the Chocolate Factory*, David worried about Oompa Loompas rolling him away as a blueberry. He writes using fat crayons.

Metamorphosis

William R. Platt

William is the current president of the Suncoast Writers Guild. He writes speculative fiction published in several anthologies, including Collections 14, 15 & 16.

Cathy Rebhun

Cathy has had short pieces published by *Reader's Digest* and *The Florida Writer* magazine. She's won several RPLA awards for her short stories.

Susan V. Rivelli

Susan is retired and living in Palm Harbor, Florida, where she enjoys spending time with family, writing, traveling, staying involved in her church, and participating in 5Ks.

K. L. Small

K. L. writes cozy fantasy for the young and young at heart. She lives in Brooksville on a horse ranch called Carousel Acres.

David Speigel

David is a retired engineer and physician, a transplant to Florida from Boston and coastal Maine and, more recently, a tentative student scribbler.

Minda A. Stephens

Minda is a lifelong Floridian currently living in Winter Park. Her writing specialties include historical and comedy scriptwriting, children's literature, copywriting, and editing.

K. M. Stull

K.M. lives in Southwest Florida with an emptying nest and a few WIPs. She currently supports school counselors for a living.

Mike Summers

Mike's upbringing with rocket fuel and dynamite led to innovation in global tech labs. His tales reflect experiences from Silicon Valley and his vivid imagination.

Metamorphosis

Lynn Taylor

Lynn holds a degree in English/Creative Writing, has won awards for her short stories and essays, and recently completed her first novel.

Ed N. White

Ed is the creator of the middle-grade mystery series *Miss Demeanor* and the author of *Taking Care*, published by Histria Books.

Sylvia Whitman

Sylvia teaches at Ringling College. Her books include *If You Meet the Devil, Don't Shake Hands* and *Decide & Survive: Pompeii*.

Robin Zabel

Robin is a retired attorney currently working on a series of short stories based on her childhood in Africa and Europe.

NextGen Contributors: Ages 9–17

Perla Anderson

Perla likes to surf, wakeboard, hang out with her friends, and draw in her spare time.

Jace Burke

Jace is a 13-year-old boy from Florida. He enjoys football, his best friends, and BBQ food. He also likes writing.

Grayson Carpel

Grayson is in 5th grade and attends Spark Hybrid Education Center in Naples, FL. Grayson enjoys school, soccer, and playing with his two dogs.

Sydney Crane

Sydney is a senior and AP Literature student from Holy Trinity Episcopal Academy. She will be attending Florida State University in the fall.

Metamorphosis

Ebelle Imani Creve-Coeur

Ebelle is a skilled, hard-working student and dancer. She has performed in Spain and at the Moscow Ballet's annual Nutcracker performance.

Reece Hemmett

Reece,13, attends Spark Hybrid Ed Center as a homeschooler. Reece loves basketball and is a knockdown shooter.

McKayla Lindor

McKayla is an excellent writer. She enjoys writing poems in her free time.

Hudson Lowe

Hudson is the oldest of three children, loves playing outdoors, anything and everything about math and science, SPARK Hybrid Education Center, and his calculator.

Collection 16

Madeline Pesi

Madeline is a student from Melbourne, Florida, graduating from Holy Trinity Episcopal Academy. She plans to attend Auburn University in the fall.

Zayba Zafar

Zayba is a passionate teen writer and volleyball player with a sharp wit. A kind-hearted and ambitious thinker with dreams of success to positively impact the world.

Acknowledgements

Let me first extend my sincerest appreciation to all the *Metamorphosis* contributors—our membership is a diverse and talented group of writers. I would also like to thank our 2024 editorial team of Rick Bettencourt, Linda Courtwright, Michael Farrell, Patricia Grayson, Linda Kraus, and David Pearce; they all worked diligently to select the best of the best submissions.

Thank you to the Collection 16 committee of Ginnye Cubel, Mary Ann de Stefano, and Michael Farrell, and Florida Writers Association's Board of Directors—you all served as a sounding board for the million-and-one ideas that floated through my head as I edited this book.

A special thanks to Carol Faber, associate professor of Graphic Design at Iowa State University, for her unique cover design; it was as if she could see into my mind's eye to draw out the image I wanted for our 2024 book cover.

And, again this year, thank you to Arielle Haughee at Orange Blossom Publishing for her formatting services and for bringing this book to print.

It has been my pleasure to serve as executive editor and my honor to work with all of you.

Paul Iasevoli, Collection 16 Executive Editor